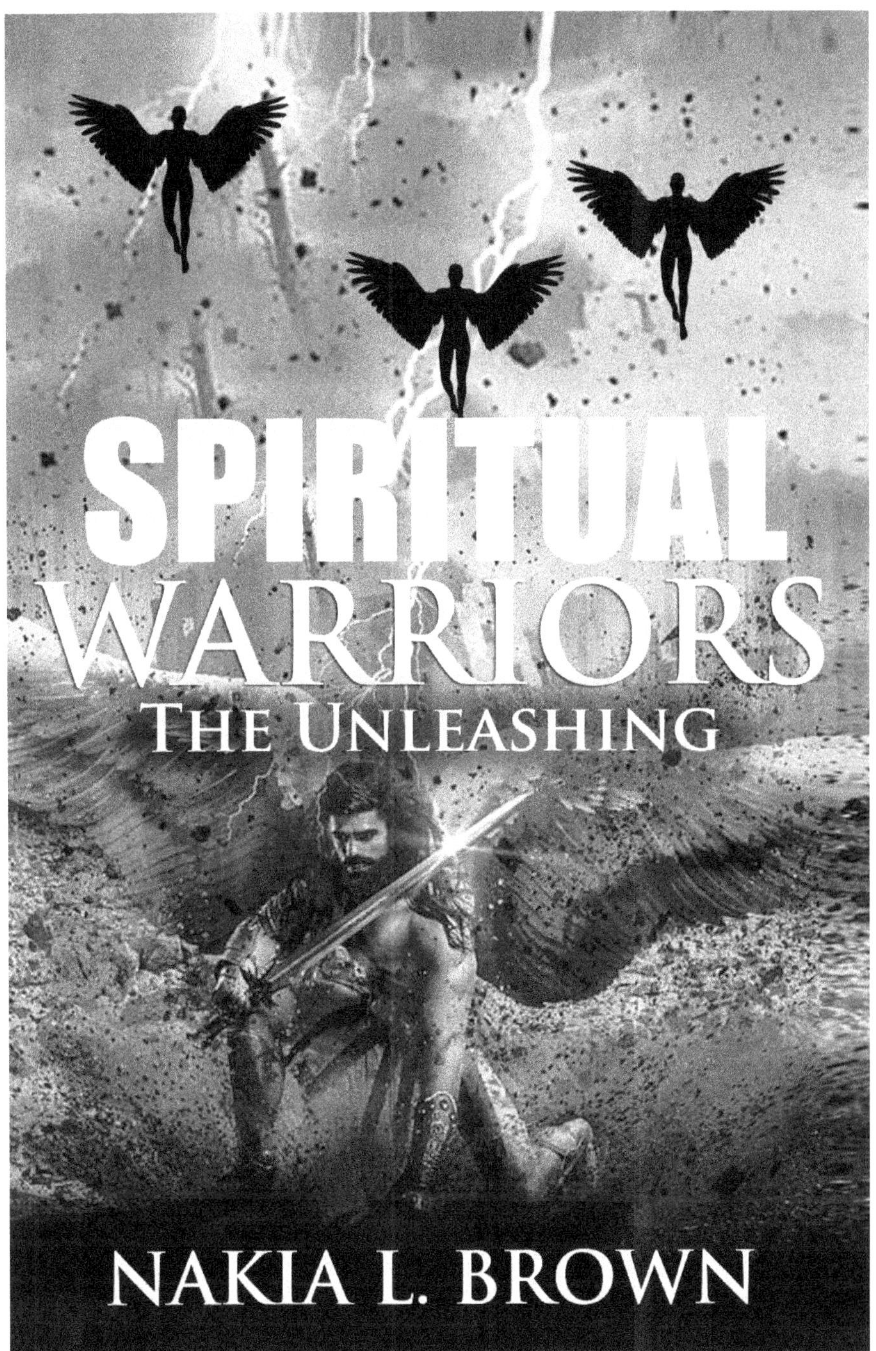
SPIRITUAL
WARRIORS
THE UNLEASHING
NAKIA L. BROWN

SPIRITUAL WARRIORS

The Unleashing

Nakia L. Brown

Pearly Gates Publishing, LLC, Houston, Texas

Spiritual Warriors:
The Unleashing

Print ISBN 13: 978-1-948853-10-1
Digital ISBN 13: 978-1-948853-11-8
Library of Congress Control Number: 2020920375

This is a work of fiction. Names, characters, businesses, places, events, locales, and incidents are either the products of the author's imagination or used in a fictitious manner.
Any resemblance to actual persons, living or dead, or actual events is purely coincidental.

Scriptures reference is taken from the Holy Bible, Amplified Version, and used with permission via Zondervan at Biblegateway.com.
Public Domain.

For information and bulk ordering, contact:
Pearly Gates Publishing, LLC
Angela Edwards, CEO
P.O. Box 62287
Houston, TX 77205
BestSeller@PearlyGatesPublishing.com

DEDICATIONS

In loving memory of:

Louis Brown
Charlene Brown
Tenisha Danielle Dubose
Shawn Dean Hamilton (aka Troy)
Jeraldine Twitty
Brenda Brown
James Hamilton, Jr.
Terry Lynn Dixon
and
Ronnie Stafford Owens

FROM SPIRITUAL WARRIORS: THE RISE OF NIGHT, THE RISE OF LIGHT

****

CHAPTER FORTY-ONE
Safe...For the Moment

On the buses, everyone witnessed the huge explosion. Alision tried contacting Benaiah and Ahijah. "Hey, guys: Are you okay? We were worried you would be caught up in the blast."

"It was close," replied Ahijah. "Hey! Tell Micah and Lanoone that Josh was the one who saved us. He changed at the end."

"Really?" Alision said happily. "Is he there with you?"

"No. He stayed behind and fought off the hounds so that we could get away."

Nagi said, "I'm sorry, guys. But you helped him change when it mattered the most."

One of the kids in the jeep suddenly yelled, "Look over there! That black fog is coming! IT'S COMING!"

Benaiah drove the jeep as fast as he could, pushing it past its normal limits, attempting to outrun the fog. Ahijah said, "It's coming right at us. There's no way we can outrun it."

Elisha said, "Guys, use your spiritual powers so that I can connect with you. I'm going to use my spirit barrier."

Nagi asked, "Can you reach them that far away?"

Elisha thought about it. "How far away are you?"

"I don't know," replied Benaiah. "We can't be too far."

Tommy shouted, "IT'S RIGHT ON US!"

Elisha heard him. "Use your spiritual powers NOW! I'm going to send the barrier!"

As the black fog closed in on them, everyone started screaming hysterically. Everything started getting very dark. Then, the Spiritual Warriors started glowing, with a bright light radiating from their bodies. The kids looked at the sight before them in amazement. From across the miles, Elisha spread her arms out, and a beam of light shot out from her hands — a light that hit all of the buses and made a beeline straight to the jeep. The fog was just about to overtake the jeep when Elisha's beam of light hit and placed a barrier around it, knocking the black fog away. No matter how hard it tried, the fog could not penetrate the barrier.

"We are safe now…at least for the moment," Elisha stated. "Do not stop driving, though. Keep heading North and try to stay on back roads."

Sarah was curious about that command. "Why is that?"

Alision said, "You will soon see. The sun is about to set."

CHAPTER FORTY-TWO
The Battle for Humanity Begins

There were places in the world that were not yet affected by the black fog. The people watched on television or listened to the radio as the reporters talked about a strange phenomenon that was taking place. People were saying that it was either a sign of the times or end of times. The Weather Channel was surveilling the fog by satellite, reporting that it was something no one has ever seen before.

The black fog was rising and spreading rapidly. Within a few hours, it was sure to cover the entire planet. Nowhere was safe—not even the boats out in the sea.

The crew on the same naval ship that first encountered the Spiritual Warriors watched as the black fog rose from the sea, heading for them. The captain said, "If anyone needs to call your loved ones, you better do it now…and pray. God be with us." Shortly after, the black fog covered all of the ships and boats at sea.

When the sun set and night fell, horrifying screams filled the air.

Everyone on the buses, along with those in the jeep, fell silent.

"What was that?" Sarah asked.

"THAT is why we can't stop. THAT is why we have to take the back roads. Those whom the fog has overcome have been consumed and are now demons," Alision explained.

Elisha said, "This is an invasion."

As the arks departed from the island to other countries around the world, everyone could hear the sounds of demons rising as the gates of Hell were opened.

"An invasion? What's happening, Elisha?" asked Sarah.

"Hell has launched its attack on all of humanity. This is just the beginning."

In the jeep, Ahijah and Benaiah looked at each other as they heard the sounds of horror floating through the still, nighttime air. The kids were absolutely terrified and sat in silence as the jeep bumped along the road. Ahijah broke the deafening silence. "It's truly us against the world now, huh, Benaiah?"

"It's about to get worse."

They fell silent again. Nobody said a word as the horrifying sounds continued, coming from all sides. All the Spiritual Warriors knew the worst was yet to come.

Somewhere, far, far away, Eziah watched as the whole world became night all at once — a true phenomenon in and of itself because the sun had been darkened as well. "Get ready, my Spiritual Warriors; for the war is here, and the battle for humanity has begun."

INTRODUCTORY BIBLE PASSAGE ABOUT "THE END TIMES"

Luke 21:7-28 Amplified Bible (AMP)

"They asked Him, "Teacher, when will these things happen? And what will be the sign when these things are about to happen?" He said, "Be careful and see to it that you are not misled; for many will come in My name [appropriating for themselves the name Messiah which belongs to Me alone], saying, 'I am He,' and 'The time is near!' Do not follow them. When you hear of wars and disturbances [civil unrest, revolts, uprisings], do not panic; for these things must take place first, but the end will not come immediately."

Things to Come

"Then Jesus told them, "Nation will rise against nation and kingdom against kingdom. There will be violent earthquakes, and in various places famines and [deadly and devastating] pestilences (plagues, epidemics); and there will be terrible sights and great signs from Heaven. But before all these things, they will lay their hands on you and will persecute you, turning you over to the synagogues and prisons, and bringing you before kings and governors for My name's sake. This will be a time and an opportunity for you to testify [about Me]. So, make up your minds not to prepare beforehand to defend yourselves; for I will give you [skillful] words and wisdom which none of your opponents will be able to resist or refute. But you will be betrayed and handed over even by parents and brothers and relatives and friends, and they will put some of you to death, and you will be continually hated by everyone because of [your association with] My name. But not a hair of your head will perish. By your [patient] endurance [empowered by the Holy

Spirit] you will gain your souls. But when you see Jerusalem surrounded by [hostile] armies, then understand [with confident assurance] that her complete destruction is near. At that time, those who are in Judea must flee to the mountains, and those who are inside the city (Jerusalem) must get out, and those who are [out] in the country must not enter the city; for these are days of vengeance [of rendering full justice of satisfaction], so that all things which are written will be fulfilled. Woe to those women who are pregnant and to those who are nursing babies in those days! For great trouble and anguish will be on the land, and wrath and retribution on this people [Israel]. And they will fall by the edge of the sword and will be led captive into all nations; and Jerusalem will be trampled underfoot by the Gentiles until the times of the Gentiles are fulfilled [completed].

The Return of Christ

"There will be signs (attesting miracles) in the sun and moon and stars; and on the earth [there will be] distress and anguish among nations, in perplexity at the roaring and tossing of the sea and the waves, people fainting from fear and expectation of the [dreadful] things coming on the world; for the [very] powers of the heavens will be shaken. Then they will see the Son of Man coming in a cloud with [transcendent, overwhelming] power [subduing the nations] and with great glory. Now when these things begin to occur, stand tall and lift up your heads [in joy], because [suffering ends as] your redemption is drawing near."

May the Lord add a blessing to the readers and doers of His Word.
Amen.

PROLOGUE

It's been almost two years since Hell declared war on humanity, releasing darkness over the land and decimating over 70% of the world's population. Many were affected by a mysterious fog that turned them into night creepers or soldiers of darkness.

The gates of Hell are now wide open. "The Unleashing" has arrived.

Now that the war has begun, the other warriors left on the island have officially been called into battle, led by Anna, Eion, Sonya, and Gadin. Each has their own special teams on the battle arks with unique weaponry and gears that were designed by angels and made by Jowel. With his intellectual gifts, he helped the others develop special suits and weapons — something that was quite out of character for him, but he knew those things would give the warriors the ability to fight the evil they would soon face.

Not too long after everyone made their departure on their respective arks, they intercepted a distress call from a naval ship.

"Hey, there's a distress call coming in," said William.

"Put it through," replied Anna.

Once the crackling from the weak signal subsided, a booming voice came through. "Hello! Can anyone hear me? This is Captain Stevenson. My crew and I are in trouble. We are trapped. Most of my men are acting strangely. It must be some type of chemical that's causing this. Can anyone hear me? Mayday! Mayday! We are in desperate need of assistance!"

William broke the silence that followed. "What do we do?"

Sonya contacted Anna, who was on another ark. "Anna, we're all going to head to that naval ship, just in case it's a trap."

"I agree. Let's go." Anna then made direct contact with the ship's captain. "Hello. This is Anna. We hear you and are on the way to your location."

"Thank you, Anna," said a relieved Captain Stevenson.

As the arks approached the ships at sea, they immediately noticed how eerily quiet it was. The waters were filled with battleships of all sizes. It looked as if it were a graveyard for ships.

"Whoa," whispered Tasha. "Talk about eerie…"

"Listen, we don't know what we are going to run into. I sense a lot of negative energy here. We may be too late to help. Don't be surprised if there are no survivors," said Gadin.

Sonya spoke up to give some directions. "He's right, so let's all be on our guard. We will each take a small team to investigate each ship here. Anna, you and your team, go and search for the captain who sent that distress call. Hopefully, he's still alive."

Anna and a handful of her team — Keemah, Comfort, William, Mizzy, and Gala — left to check the ship for the captain and other survivors. "Let's split up into two teams. We can cover more ground that way," Anna directed. Anna, Mizzy, and Keemah went in one direction, while Comfort, William, and Gala went in the other.

Mizzy spoke first. "I'm picking up all kinds of negative energy but no movement."

"Probably because it's not dark yet," replied Keemah.

"We need to try and hurry to find survivors before it gets dark," said Anna. She then contacted the others. "Guys, beware. Once it gets dark, the ships are going to swarming with night creepers."

"Gotcha," said Gala. "We have not found a single survivor yet."

"If we stay until it gets dark, we will probably face 300 to 400 night creepers. We do not have much room to fight that many," said William, his voice filled with concern.

"Is the captain still alive?" asked Comfort.

"Yes," Anna replied. "I can still feel just a few positive energy sources in this place, so they must be close."

"We have less than an hour to find them before we end up in a close encounter combat situation," said Keemah.

Eion's voice came through the walkie-talkies. "Sis, how's the recovery mission going?"

"We're still searching, Eion," replied Anna. "We want to be sure we don't miss anyone."

"Oh. Okay. Well, we found no one. I can't detect any positive energy anywhere. We're going to make another sweep and then head back to our ark. Don't stay there too long. It's going to get dark soon, and I know how you are," said Eion.

Anna let out a soft giggle. "I know."

"Your brother is right," Sonya chimed in. "Once it's dark, we're going to have to destroy all the ships."

With the sun setting unusually fast, the warriors knew their time was running out. Just as they were preparing to leave, Anna suddenly sensed a host of positive energies. "Gala, I think I found them. Meet us on the third deck."

"Roger. We are on our way."

As Gala and the others made their way to where Anna and the others were, Mizzy began detecting negative energy movement. "I sense movement. There's a lot of them." Just as she finished her sentence, Gala and the others showed up.

"There's movement heading this way," said William.

Anna yelled, "Weapons up! Let's hurry to the survivors!"

As the group made their way, they found themselves cornered by night creepers. They had no choice but to engage them in battle, all while fighting their way to the survivors. Anna heard some of them crying out for help, which drew the attention of some of the nigh creepers. They turned and tried to violently bust into the locked room. At the same time, the warriors heard the teams fighting on the other ships.

"Anna, get out of there…NOW!" screamed Gadin.

"No! We can't leave now! We found the survivors!"

"Anna, go get them. We'll hold off these monsters," yelled Keemah.

At that moment, a desperate voice came floating through the air. "Is anyone out there? Please hurry! They are going to break in!"

Anna took off running towards them. As soon as the night creepers sensed her presence, they turned around and began attacking her. It didn't take Anna long to destroy the beasts. The survivors heard the commotion and then noticed how quiet it was on the other side of the door. Anna then ripped the door off its hinges. "Is everyone okay?"

Captain Stevenson stepped forward and said, "Yes, thanks to you." He leaned his head to the side before speaking again. "You are like the ones we saw before all of this happened."

"'Like the ones you saw,'" Anna repeated in confusion.

Before the captain could respond, Mizzy contacted Anna. "We better hurry and get out of here!"

"Okay! I have them with me. They're safe. We're on the way!" Anna replied. She then turned to the captain and other survivors. "Stay close, everyone. We're getting out of here. Follow me."

The crew hesitated and turned to the captain for direction. "You heard her! Stay close!"

As the group approached an exit, Comfort was there, fighting a host of night creepers. "They're coming at me from both directions!" she yelled.

Anna had to think quickly. She punched a hole in a nearby wall and instructed the captain and his crew to go through to the other side. No one moved, obviously scared of what could possibly be awaiting them. She turned to Captain Stevenson and spoke with surety. "Sir, you and your crew can follow my friends. I promise to be right behind you."

The group did as they were told and headed to the top deck, soon to board the warriors' ark. At the top, Eion, Sonya, and Gadin waited patiently for Anna. The others didn't know Eion was having a conversation with himself.

"Trust in your sister, Eion… Come on, sis… Get out of there…"

Anna fought off a few more night creepers, went through the hole after the others, and resealed it so the beasts couldn't break through.

"Gala, is everyone on the ark?" asked Anna.

"Yes."

"Good. Tell everyone else to start pulling away and prepare to fire on the ships that are in the way."

Captain Stevenson noticed Anna did not board the ark with them. "Are you going to leave her behind? You can't do that!"

"Sir, with all due respect, Anna knows what she's doing. We all trust her. Plus, she is one of our team leaders. Trust me: She will be okay," Gala confidently replied.

"How?" asked the captain.

Keemah walked up to him, put a hand on his shoulder, and said, "Just watch. You will see, sir."

TABLE OF CONTENTS

Dedications vi

From Spiritual Warriors: The Rise of Night, The Rise of Light.................. vii

Introductory Bible Passage About "The End Times" xi

Prologue.. xiii

CHAPTER ONE 1

    Cutting It Close

CHAPTER TWO 4

    Absolute Faith

CHAPTER THREE 6

    Promotion and Acceptance

CHAPTER FOUR 8

    Being on Guard

CHAPTER FIVE..10

    Eion and the Ruffnecks

CHAPTER SIX...11

    Fear of the Fog

CHAPTER SEVEN 14

    Lives Transformed

CHAPTER EIGHT...20

    Laughter is Good for the Soul

CHAPTER NINE..22

    A Flood of Memories

CHAPTER TEN 25

    Stranger Danger

CHAPTER ELEVEN 27

    The Innocents

CHAPTER TWELVE 29

Give Him What He Wants

CHAPTER THIRTEEN 30

One-on-One Combat

CHAPTER FOURTEEN 31

Talking Back

CHAPTER FIFTEEN 34

The Legion Brothers

CHAPTER SIXTEEN 35

He Will Rise

CHAPTER SEVENTEEN..38

Before I Go

CHAPTER EIGHTEEN 39

The Darkest on Earth

CHAPTER NINETEEN 41

Major Losses

CHAPTER TWENTY 43

This Is Not A Drill

CHAPTER TWENTY-ONE 46

The Oldest Demons

CHAPTER TWENTY-TWO...48

A Legendary Saint

CHAPTER TWENTY-THREE 49

They Keep Coming

CHAPTER TWENTY-FOUR 52

Firebirds

CHAPTER TWENTY-FIVE...54

Swiftness and Timeliness

CHAPTER TWENTY-SIX 56

You Don't Want A Piece of This

CHAPTER TWENTY-SEVEN.. 57

Don't Look Back

CHAPTER TWENTY-EIGHT 61

What's Your Position?

CHAPTER TWENTY-NINE 63

Uncomfortable Feelings

CHAPTER THIRTY 64

A Sense of Worry

CHAPTER THIRTY-ONE 65

Going Unnoticed

CHAPTER THIRTY-TWO 66

Preventing Utter Destruction

CHAPTER THIRTY-THREE 70

Step It Up...Pronto

CHAPTER THIRTY-FOUR 71

Out of the League

CHAPTER THIRTY-FIVE 73

Changing Course

CHAPTER THIRTY-SIX 74

Feel the Rage

CHAPTER THIRTY-SEVEN 77

Distracted...For Just A Moment

CHAPTER THIRTY-EIGHT.. 78

Nowhere Is Safe

CHAPTER THIRTY-NINE 81

The Death Stare

CHAPTER FORTY...83

A Changing Landscape

CHAPTER FORTY-ONE...84

There Are Three

CHAPTER FORTY-TWO...85

Go, Betsy! Go!

CHAPTER FORTY-THREE 87

The Ocean Speaks

CHAPTER FORTY-FOUR...88

A Familiar Feeling

CHAPTER FORTY-FIVE...89

The Flames and the Hounds

CHAPTER FORTY-SIX...94

New Friends

CHAPTER FORTY-SEVEN 101

Distress Signal

CHAPTER FORTY-EIGHT 104

It's A Trap

CHAPTER FORTY-NINE...107

The Demon-Human

CHAPTER FIFTY..110

They Can't Help

CHAPTER FIFTY-ONE..113

All the Faith

CHAPTER FIFTY-TWO...115

The Lion Returns

CHAPTER FIFTY-THREE 116

Squealing Like A Pig

CHAPTER FIFTY-FOUR 119

Great Faith

CHAPTER FIFTY-FIVE 120

The Gates Are Opening

CHAPTER FIFTY-SIX 121

Close and Accurate

CHAPTER FIFTY-SEVEN 124

Adriam and Hadeon

CHAPTER FIFTY-EIGHT 127

Battling the Fire

CHAPTER FIFTY- NINE 129

The Raging Flames

CHAPTER SIXTY.. 131

The Teams Come Together

CHAPTER SIXTY-ONE 136

It May Be the Last

CHAPTER SIXTY-TWO 138

Where There's Music

CHAPTER SIXTY-THREE 141

The Momma Witch

CHAPTER SIXTY-FOUR 142

Meet the Mate

CHAPTER SIXTY-FIVE 144

A Full Onslaught

CHAPTER SIXTY-SIX 146

They're Saved!

CHAPTER SIXTY-SEVEN 148

The Gate Is the Focus

CHAPTER SIXTY-EIGHT...149

Unleash It All

CHAPTER SIXTY-NINE 151

Angelic Vs. Evil Armor

CHAPTER SEVENTY...153

The Necessary Sacrifice

CHAPTER SEVENTY-ONE 155

Giants Return

CHAPTER SEVENTY-TWO 157

They're Coming Soon

CHAPTER SEVENTY-THREE..159

The Weak Spot

CHAPTER SEVENTY-FOUR 160

Shut It Down

CHAPTER SEVENTY-FIVE 161

Thank You for Your Service

CHAPTER SEVENTY-SIX 163

Another One Destroyed

CHAPTER SEVENTY-SEVEN..164

Two More Gone

CHAPTER SEVENTY-EIGHT 166

To the Safe Zone

CONCLUSION 168

CHAPTER ONE
Cutting It Close

The army of arks began pulling away with their weapons at the ready. Just when the captain thought all hope was lost, Anna came running full speed toward the ark. Eion watched his sister with a smile on his face. He knew then like he knew before:

Anna can definitely handle her own!

"FIRE!" Anna yelled. "FIRE NOW!"

On cue, all the arks began firing at the ships.

"There's no way she will make that jump. We're at least 100 yards away," said the captain.

Anna continued to run towards the end of the ship. Just as the first missile struck, she jumped onto the ark with ease. The captain and crew were shocked and amazed.

"I told you," said Gala.

Anna walked up to them and asked, "Are you all okay?" None spoke. They just continued looking at her in amazement and shook their heads in the affirmative.

Anna and the other warriors on all the arks watched as the ships exploded and began sinking to the bottom, killing all the night creepers in the process.

"You like cutting it close, don't you?" Sonya said with a smile.

"Sorry about that, Sonya." Anna returned the smile and then turned to Captain Stevenson. "Sir, I am sorry for the loss of your crew and the ships, but we had to destroy them. Your people were no longer human. They turned into soldiers of darkness. Please follow me. There are some people I want you to meet. Plus, I know you have a lot of questions."

Before they all went their separate ways again, Anna introduced the captain to the other team leaders. "Guys, this is Captain Stevenson. This is my twin brother, Eion. These two are my teachers, Gadin and Sonya. There's another, but he's not here at the moment. His name is Eziah."

"It's nice to meet all of you. Thank you for saving our lives," replied the captain.

"It's an honor, sir," Sonya said. "We're sorry we couldn't save all the others."

"You must have a lot of questions," stated Gadin matter-of-factly.

"Yes, I do, with my first being: Are you all like her?" he asked, pointing to Anna.

"Yes, we are," replied Gadin.

"My crew and I saw others like you when this all began."

"Really?!" asked Eion. "You must have seen Nagi and the others."

The captain shook his head from side to side as he recalled the moment. "It was something I have never seen before. There were eight of them. They ran past us atop the water like a jet. Well, actually faster than a jet. We didn't know what to do or think. We tried to attack them; however, they disappeared out of sight. It was as if in the blink of an eye, they were gone!"

"They were our brothers and sisters you attacked," said Anna, her voice testy.

"Easy, Anna," coaxed Sonya. "He didn't know what was happening."

"I'm very sorry," Captain Stevenson said sincerely. "I don't know what's going on. All I recall is seeing black smoke rising all around. Then, many of my crew began to change right before my eyes."

"Captain, do you believe in Heaven and Hell, angels and demons, God and Satan?" asked Gadin.

"I mean…I believe in God, but probably not as much as I should."

Gadin continued. "The black smoke you saw was not actually smoke. It was a host of demons, looking for hosts to possess."

"You mean to tell me that smoke was demon-filled?!"

"Yes, but that's not the only source," replied Anna. "There are a whole lot more in the shadows."

Captain Stevenson was obviously confused.

"Sir, in other words, Hell has unleashed war upon humanity," Sonya tried to explain.

"And we are going into battle to stop them," added Eion.

CHAPTER TWO
Absolute Faith

As was his nature, Captain Stevenson listened intently to everything the warriors said. Although what they stated raised the hairs on the back of his neck and almost overwhelmed him, he found himself understanding the severity of their discussion. "So, I can never return home?" he asked

"No. I'm afraid not, sir," Gadin confirmed. "Did you have anyone in your life back home in the United States?"

"No. Being on ships kept me kinda alone. The crew members became my family."

"Sorry, sir," Gadin said sincerely.

"It's okay. So, what now?"

Sonya breathed deeply before responding. "We are about to go battle against evil in different countries, as well as see if there are any other survivors."

"What are my crew members and I supposed to do?"

"Unfortunately, you will have to come with us." Gadin's tone was both serious and sorrowful.

"No disrespect, but we are still soldiers," Captain Stevenson said proudly. "We would like to fight, too, if it's to save what's left of humanity."

"The more, the merrier!" Gadin exclaimed. "We would be honored to have you fight along with us."

Anna smiled when she said, "You and your guys can come with us onto our ark."

"Okay! That's fine with me!"

Before departing, everyone said their goodbyes, unsure of what the future held but believing God would protect them.

As brother and sister embraced in a hug, Eion said to Anna, "Stay safe, sis, and watch yourself out there."

"I will. You do the same. I love you, bro."

Sonya and Gadin told them both to remember their training and to always trust in their team. "When the time is right, we will see each other again. We have absolute faith in each of you," Gadin said as the leaders gave each other a fist bump.

Everyone boarded their ark with their respective crew and "new members," then headed off in different directions to battle the unknown forces of darkness.

CHAPTER THREE
Promotion and Acceptance

After spending a year aboard the ark with Anna and her team and observed what they fought, Captain Stevenson began to understand more about what he was told concerning the evil that overtook the world. All the while, he learned all he could about the ark, which proved fruitful because it was agreed that he could become an Admiral.

Anna explained why they chose him for the task: "You already know everything about the seas and various ships. You know the ark inside and out, and about the war we are fighting. It's befitting that we make and call you Admiral Stevenson. I know it may not be the proper way to do it, but under the current circumstances…" Her voice trailed off.

"I don't know what to say. I am humbly grateful."

"Say you accept!" Anna said with a wide smile.

"Okay! I accept!" said now-Admiral Stevenson.

Everyone on the ark broke out into loud applause. Even the ones on the other arks nearby heard and joined in with their congratulatory shouts. Eion, Gadin, and Sonya congratulated him, saying, "You earned it, sir."

Anna went on to further explain Admiral Stevenson's duties. "So, when I'm not here, all responsibilities are on you."

"Are you sure? I haven't been with you as long as the others."

"I'm sure," Anna confirmed. "There's a reason why we found you. God has a plan for you, and, in time, you will know what it is."

Admiral Stevenson looked at her with a look of pride.

CHAPTER FOUR
Being on Guard

Two years into the war, the warriors rarely encountered heavy attacks or had any casualties on their missions. As it turned out, many of the smaller countries and islands were overrun with evil. The only way to close the gates of Hell was to eradicate any existing evils present.

"Hey, guys! How are things going with the mission?" asked Anna as she contacted the other arks.

"Okay, I guess," replied Eion. "We had some successful missions in Germany and France. Now, we are on the way to where we spent the last time with our parents in London."

"Be careful, bro," Anna stated with concern.

"I will, sis. You know me!"

"Yeah, I know! That's why I said to be careful. As for us, we had some success in Asia. Now, we're off to Africa. We never really ran into anything heavy. Something's not right with that, though."

"You're right, Anna," Gadin said. "Something is definitely not right."

Sonya chimed in. "Up to this point, none of us have experienced a heavy attack. I sense something really big is coming our way."

"We all must be on our guard. As for us, we are on our way to South America," replied Gadin.

"And we are on our way to the Netherlands. Every now and then, try to stay in touch. Until we get back together, may God be with us all," Sonya stated as she bowed her head.

"Wait! Has anyone heard anything about the others in the States?" asked Anna. "I haven't been able to reach them since this all began. I'm worried."

Gadin spoke up with confidence. "Don't worry. I'm sure they are doing okay. Remember: There's a lot of negative energy out there blocking our communication, but we would know if something was wrong nonetheless."

"He's right, sis. You know they can handle anything that comes their way," Eion said assuredly.

"Yeah. You're right. Okay. You all take care out there!"

"Don't worry, Anna," Sonya said. "You will see them again soon.

At that, all communication stopped, and the missions were resumed.

CHAPTER FIVE
Eion and the Ruffnecks

After a successful mission in France and Germany of finding survivors, Eion and his team called the Ruffnecks made their way to England—the country where Eion and Anna first encountered evil. The mission wasn't going to be as easy as the others because he knew something very evil and powerful was waiting for them.

"Okay, guys. We're about to reach England. You all heard me when I was talking to my sister and told her that so far, we hadn't really had too many instances of heavy resistance. There's something wrong with that, though. So, we must be ready for whatever awaits us in England," Eion instructed.

Tasha spun around in a circle slowly while saying, "I detect on my radar a lot of signs of life here."

"Nothing has changed," Eion replied. "We must try to save every survivor you detect on your scanners. Remember: If your scanners detect any other color than white, you know that is not a person. Jowel designed the detectors to distinguish between real humans and those that try to disguise themselves as humans. Try not to engage head-on with any necromancers. Use your scanners all the time, as they can pick up strong, dark energy signatures." As the ark reached the England waters, Eion said, "Okay. We are here. Everyone be safe. May God be with us." The teams then went off in different directions.

CHAPTER SIX
Fear of the Fog

Eion and his team started in the countryside.

Tasha said, "Wow. It's so foggy. I can barely see a thing."

"That's what worries me," Eion agreed. "The fog is blocking the sunlight."

"Well, I detect survivors just a few miles ahead," Tasha stated. "I also detect something else coming toward us."

"I sense it, too. Night creepers are coming. Everyone, get your weapons ready!"

Before the team knew it, night creepers broke through the fog. They began firing from their vehicles at the night creepers.

"Go find cover while I hold them off!" yelled Eion.

"No way!" yelled Crae Crae. "You know better than that! We're not leaving you alone!"

"Grr! This stupid fog! Everyone brace yourself! It's about to get windy!" Eion screamed. As his eyes began to glow, he started twirling his weapon in the air really fast and then struck the ground hard, causing a powerful force to unleash a mighty wind that blew away the fog. The sun shone down on them, causing the night creepers to scatter.

"They are fleeing!" Tasha exclaimed happily.

"Yeah, but not for long. We must hurry and find the survivors before it gets dark," Eion stated. As the team continued onward, Eion's uneasy feeling grew.

Once they reached the survivors, they were understandably too scared to come outside.

"They are scared," Tasha said.

"Can you blame them?" Crae Crae asked. "After what happened and what's out here now, I would be, too, if I were them."

Tasha spoke to the fearful people. "It's okay. We are here to help you. We are not like them."

As the team tried to convince them it was okay to come out, a few others said they would scout out the area to see what was up ahead.

"Okay, but don't stay gone too long," Eion said.

"We have to find shelter soon. The sun is setting," Tasha observed.

Just as they were getting everyone prepared to move, one of the team members returned and said, "There's a big building up ahead that looks like a school of some sort."

"That's great! We can go there for the night," Eion said. "Wait. I sense something approaching us."

Another team member ran up to the group and said, "There's a pack of hounds a few miles away heading this way."

"Okay, everyone. We must get out of here quickly. We cannot afford to fight right now. We have civilians with us," Eion said.

The team and survivors quickly made their way towards the old building—with the hounds right on their trail.

CHAPTER SEVEN
Lives Transformed

When the group arrived at the building, they found out some people were already hiding out in there.

Eion told them, "It's okay. We are not here to hurt you. We are here to help. However, there's danger heading this way. We need to get everyone inside before the hounds get to us." He then used a device to try and throw the hounds off their trail and told everyone to remain silent. He could hear and sense the hounds and other evil beings fastly approaching.

The team watched as the hounds went right by them. Nonetheless, they had their weapons ready should something go wrong. A short time passed before they heard the screams of the night creepers that had come together in a large group. At one point, a group the size of an army passed them by. One of the creepers stopped and looked in their direction.

"They can't see us, right?" Tasha asked.

Eion responded by saying, "No, but I think it senses something is different. Just be ready."

The night creeper suddenly turned away and resumed walking with the others like it.

"They are heading towards London," Eion observed. "I sense a lot of survivors are there."

"You are right," Tasha agreed. "I, too, detect a lot."

Eion looked around and then back at the group of survivors. "They know we will be coming, and something will definitely be waiting for us when we arrive. Unfortunately, there's nothing we can do tonight. We must wait until the morning when the rescue team gets here to get these people to the ark."

"Hey, Eion. How does it feel to be back here after all this time?" Tasha asked.

"To be honest, it feels kinda weird. If it weren't for Teacher Eziah saving us, my sis and I wouldn't be here. It took a while for us to come to terms with what happened."

"Who would have thought we would be at war with evil spirits, demons, and only Lord knows what else?" Tasha shared her innermost thoughts aloud.

"Yeah. I know, but we better try to get some rest. I'll take the first watch," Eion suggested.

After a couple of hours, Tasha found she couldn't rest, so she got up and went over to Eion.

"What's wrong?" he asked.

"I just can't rest. It's hard to do with everything that's going on."

"I understand."

They fell silent and listened to the sounds around them. Throughout the night, sounds of creatures could be heard near and far.

"Listen to that. It used to be the sounds of crickets and other normal night creatures. Now, it's that," Eion said irritably. He turned to look around at everyone in their newly-formed group and saw Crae Crae playing with the kids.

"It's hard to believe that years ago, Crae Crae was as bad as they come," Tasha said.

"Really?" Eion asked with a little giggle in his voice.

"Yep! Actually, most of us were totally different people back then."

"How so?" Eion's curiosity piqued.

"Well, most of us had a bad past. A lot of us were heading down a dark road. Were it not for Eziah, Gadin, and Sonya, you would probably be fighting us, too. I'm telling you, back then, I didn't care about anything or anyone but me. I wasn't a very nice person at all. I was always ready to fight someone until I saw evil with my own eyes. What I witnessed scared me straight! I guess it was meant for me to see it because, after that, something started to change in me. I kept having nightmares, and soon after, I was approached by them. They told me it wasn't too late and that everyone deserved a second chance. Then, Eziah touched my head. Since then, I haven't had a bad dream. They then took me to the island where there were others like me who wanted a second chance and whose pasts were terrible. That's how I met Crae Crae and the others. Do you know that all of us on the island are a lot older than you all?"

Eion turned to look at her. "Huh? How is that?"

"Well, they told us the island was blessed by God and that once you came, depending on your age, it gave us the gift of longevity. If you were young when you came, you age normally until you reach a certain age. Then, your aging slows down. But, if you are already that age or older, your aging completely stops."

"It's because it would take years for all of us to be ready. God has a purpose for everyone until that purpose is fulfilled."

"Wow!" Eion exclaimed. "None of us realized or thought about it like that. That's why we never said anything."

"So, how old are most of you? I'm going to guess around 90 years old?"

"Crae and I are in our 50s. Insane, I know. Craig—or Crae Crae, as we know him—told me he shot people before. Luckily, nobody died. He never got caught until one day, he accidently shot a kid because he was having a shootout with another person. Once he realized what he had done, he took the kid to the hospital. The kid lived, but that moment has haunted Crae Crae. That's when he started seeing demons. He went back to the hospital and confessed to the kid's parents that it was he who shot their son and that he was turning himself into the police. He then grabbed the kid's hand, laid his head against him, and apologized for what he had done. After that, he turned and hugged the mother. The parents didn't know what to think. Crae told them to call the police and that he would be by the door of the hospital waiting. The father wasn't too happy, of course. He wanted to jump up and beat Crae down, but the mother said, 'No. Stop. He didn't have to be here, but he came.' Crae Crae then put on his headphones and started listening to music while sitting on the floor, waiting for the police to arrive. They came and arrested him. He spent five years in prison. It could have been a lot longer, but the parents told the court what he did, so the judge granted some leniency. The parents even brought their son to visit him in prison, just so Crae could see the kid was doing okay. They also told him they forgive him. Once he was released, he didn't know where to go because he was on his own, but Gadin was waiting for him and brought him to the island. Even though he's still a little crazy and wild, it's in a good way. That's why we call him Crae or Crae Crae. Eziah explained to us everything we needed to know and how everyone on the island is a new person. Even though we changed, we still kept that one part of us that helped prepare us for this moment. He also told us that one day, we would have special young people who have also been through a great ordeal. They are a vital key in the war to come, and we must welcome them. Then, years later, all of you arrived!"

Eion asked, "Do any of you regret learning about what was coming and could happen?"

"No. Not at all. We all knew what we signed up for. We wanted a purpose. The least we could do is support them. If it weren't for them, we wouldn't be here. They helped with our change and showed us a better way. When Eziah told us God would never forsake us and that He doesn't care about our past, as long as we know God forgives us, we should forgive ourselves. That's all that matters. We must move forward and be better and stronger than we were. Those very words changed all of us. We could have been fighting each other, rather than fighting together. For that, we will always be grateful."

Eion nodded his head in agreement. "I completely understand. That's how we feel, too. We are glad we met everyone. You all mean a lot to us."

Just then, Crae Crae and the rest of the team walked up to give their report. "The refugees are safe, and the wounded have been tended to. Everything is secure. Nothing is getting in here without us knowing," Crae stated confidently.

"Thanks, everyone." Eion's voice was heavy with concern. "They know we are here. Up until now, we've had no real resistance, so we must assume we will encounter a lot once we get to London."

Crae got hyped up at those words. "Oh, yeah. They know. But what they don't know is who they are going to be dealing with! We are the Ruffnecks, baby!"

The rest of the team joined in the revelry.

"Heck yeah!"

"No matter what they throw at us, we will still take them down!"

"Plus, we are all too hard-headed to know when to give up!" Crae shouted.

Eion said with a laugh, "That's for sure! Well, we better rest now. Tomorrow, we head to London."

CHAPTER EIGHT
Laughter is Good for the Soul

The next morning, the rescue team arrived on schedule. The other team members who also had survivors came as well. Eion and the others worked together to load the survivors onto the helicopters to be taken to the ark. Eion told the rescue team they would be notified once the warriors reached London. He also instructed everyone on the ark to be on standby because he and the others would definitely need their support.

Once all the survivors were secure and on their way to safety, Eion gathered the team for a pep talk. "Look, guys. This will not be an easy task. London is our last stop. There is no doubt that something will be waiting for our arrival."

Crae Crae said, "It's all good. They don't know how crazy we are!"

Everyone enjoyed a good laugh, breaking up the seriousness of the situation for just a moment.

"You got that right, Crae," Eion said, "but it will be a difficult mission. We should reach London within a day."

Crae was ready to fight! "That's okay. You know I got them beat for us!"

Someone else said, "We can always count on you to get us hyped, Crae!"

Once everyone calmed down, Tasha said, "There are a lot of survivors there."

"Yes, and they are all counting on us. Whatever comes at us, we deal with it, okay?" Eion asked, not really expecting an answer.

As they began to move out, Eion had a focused and concerned look on his face as he thought to himself, "I'm going back to where it all began for my sister and me. I know there's a strong evil presence awaiting us, but I also know my team can handle anything that comes their way."

He and the team will have to travel through the night to reach London as soon as possible. As well, they may have to fight their way there. Hours went by. The team got closer to their destination. A team member approached Eion and asked if he had heard anything from those in America.

"The last I heard, the others had to set up camp not too far from the safe zone, but I haven't heard anything since. That was a few weeks ago."

"Do you think everything is okay?" the team member asked.

"Oh, I know everything is okay." Eion didn't want to tell anyone that something powerful was blocking the leaders from communicating with each other.

CHAPTER NINE
A Flood of Memories

Eion and the team were just a few miles away from London, and night was coming. The fastest way to get there was through the town where he and Anna first encountered the evil. As they walked through, Eion had Crae Crae turn off the music he was playing so that he could hear and sense clearly. There were no lights on…anywhere. There were no survivors to help. It looked like a ghost town—something out of a scary movie. The whole town looked and felt absolutely dead, and the streets were completely black.

"Put on your night goggles," he instructed. He could see well in the dark with his spiritual eyes.

Soon, they came to the place where he and his sister came face-to-face with the evil that nearly killed them. Eion came to an immediate halt.

"What's wrong, Eion? Why did we stop?" Tasha asked.

He explained: "This is the place where my sister and I came face-to-face with what took our parents—the same thing that tried to kill us. My sister yelled and yelled for someone to help us, but everyone just shut their door on us. That was when Teacher arrived and saved us. Afterward, I was so mad at those people and had it in my mind to hate them, but Teacher sensed it right away. On the way to the island, he told me something that stuck with me: 'You must forgive them. They were afraid of what they saw and could not comprehend what was going on. Don't be mad or hate anyone for their actions.' You see, that is why God chose us to be warriors and to fight against the evil you witness. We must fight for the ones who can't fight for themselves against the fear and hatred."

The entire team listened intently and with deep thought. It was Tasha who broke the silence. "I can't imagine all that you went through, being that you were so young."

"Yeah, but some had it rougher than others. It's all good now. Let's keep moving. It looks like there's nothing here…which is odd," Eion stated.

"They are waiting for us in London," Crae Crae said.

One of the other team members who was still wearing their special night vision goggles saw a spiritual figure standing in the distance. The figure wore a hoodie that covered his eyes. "There's a spirit standing over there," he said.

"Wait here, everyone. I'll be right back," stated Eion. The team did as they were instructed, as Eion walked over to the spirit and asked for his name.

"That's not important right now. What is important is that there is a powerful demon and necromancer sorceress waiting for you in London. One of them has important information concerning events that are soon to happen, along with their plans. You must get there quickly and get the information."

"What kind of information?" Eion asked.

"That, I do not know. I can only tell you that something big is coming. I must leave."

In a flash, the spirit was gone.

Eion's obvious look of concern shone on his face as he walked back to tell the others what was told to him.

"What's going on? Who was that?" Tasha asked.

"I don't know who it was, but he told me a powerful demon and necromancer is in London waiting for us and that they hold important information about their main objectives and what's coming. We need to retrieve that information, which means we must try and save the people there and get what is waiting for us. It must be very important for a spirit to come and relay the message. This is going to be the hardest mission we have yet to face since we started. I can feel the strength of their evil presence as we speak."

Tasha then said, "You would think they're attacking the remaining survivors there."

"Yeah, we would think that," agreed Eion, "but they are hiding and waiting. All they want is us."

"Well, let's go! They know we are coming, anyway!" said Crae Crae. "I'm ready to bash some demon heads in!"

CHAPTER TEN
Stranger Danger

"Let's keep moving, team. There's nothing else here anyway. The next stop is London," Eion stated.

After traveling for hours nonstop, the team finally arrived. The city was in ruins. Tasha immediately detected a lot of survivors in hiding. "There are a lot of survivors here, but they are all hidden throughout the city."

"They are scared to come out because they know what waits in the shadows," Eion whispered.

Out of nowhere, someone came running towards them, saying, "You must go back! They know you are here!"

Eion attempted to calm down the stranger. "We know. Do not worry. We will get everyone out of here." Just then, the sky began to get cloudy. Black clouds gathered over them. As Eion looked up, he knew that only a sorceress could make that happen. "Weapons up!" he shouted. He then turned to the survivor and told him to take shelter…fast.

Another team member said, "I'm getting a bunch of negative readings coming straight at us."

"Night creepers," Crae said.

Indeed, it was night creepers coming at them like a swarm of ants. The team immediately began firing at them.

"Spread out! They are trying to surround us!" Eion shouted.

A team member asked, "Why aren't they attacking the survivors?"

"Because they want to get rid of us first!" Eion yelled. He then saw a dark figure standing in the distance, looking directly at them. He knew right away that it was the demonic leader. "I see the demon. I'm going after him to try and retrieve the information. Be on your guard. The necromancer is around here somewhere, and there may be more of them. Don't try to fight them alone."

"Okay. We gotcha," Tasha replied.

With that assurance, Eion took off running toward the demon, prepared to do battle. As he raced toward the demon, he quickly glanced back and saw the others battling the night creepers. He heard a team member yell, "They're coming from everywhere!" However, he couldn't go back. He had a fight all his own to contend with.

CHAPTER ELEVEN
The Innocents

"Stay focused!" Tasha yelled. "Keep fighting! Don't let up!"

Suddenly, some of the night creepers changed their tactics and started going towards a group of survivors that were in hiding.

Crae noticed and said, "Those jokers are going after the survivors!"

"Crae, you and a few others come with me. We must stop the beasts before they reach the innocents," Tasha yelled. As they ran, a weapon of some sort came rushing at that from the ground, greatly slowing their progress.

Crae yelled, "Look out!"

They all jumped out of the way just in time. Right before their very eyes, a figure rose from the ground…and then another. Standing in front of them and blocking their way to the survivors were two necromancers: a warrior and the sorceress. The sorceress spoke: "There's no need to be in a hurry. You can't save them. This is where you all die!"

"Really? Is that what you think?" Tasha asked with a hint of sarcasm in her voice. "We heard one of you has some information we need."

The sorceress looked at her with surprise. "How could you possibly know that?"

"Don't worry about that. From the look on your face, it would appear that you are the one with the information we need," Crae Crae said with a sneer.

The sorceress shot them a look that said, "I don't think so," but Tasha was quick to call her out on it. "Yes, you — and you are going to give it to us, even if we have to beat it out of you!" The sorceress turned to the warrior necromancer and told him to stop them.

Tasha told Crae, "Listen, we can't afford to let her slip away. I'm going after her. Y'all take care of the others."

"Tasha, remember what Eion said: Do not take on a necromancer alone."

"I know, Crae. But right now, there's no choice. We need that information."

"Okay, Tasha. Watch yourself."

"Will do. As soon as the warrior comes at us, give me an opening."

"I got you."

Just as expected, the warriors came at them, which gave Crae the opportunity to make way for Tasha to go after the sorceress.

As Tasha and sorceress collided, Tasha yelled, "It's you and me, witch!"

CHAPTER TWELVE
Give Him What He Wants

Meanwhile, Eion met face-to-face with the demon leader for a showdown. As they faced off, the demon spoke. "I have been waiting for you. We could have killed all these people before your arrival. What fun that would have been. But I also knew we had to get rid of you first in order to complete our mission. I heard stories about your kind, so it will be fulfilling to be the first to kill one of you."

"Your words mean nothing to me. I'm here to destroy you, plain and simple — and get the information I need from you."

The demon laughed, saying, "Information? What makes you think I have any type of information? What makes you think I would even give it to you? Destroy me? Ha! We shall see about that, flesh boy." At that, the demon charged towards Eion.

Eion rose his staff and began clashing with the demon. Eion hit the demon multiple times, sending it flying into a pile of rocks. "What is about to happen?" he screamed.

The demon rose and said, "Don't get cocky, boy. You haven't defeated me. Boy, you have no idea who you are dealing with. I am one of the legions, boy with blackness swirling around him!"

"I don't care what you say! You will give me what I came for!" Eion's eyes began to glow, and his staff transformed into a spear.

CHAPTER THIRTEEN
One-on-One Combat

Meanwhile, Tasha is having a hard time fighting the sorceress. The witch keeps using her telekinetic abilities to send objects flying at her.

"This crazy witch is getting on my last nerve! I can't get close to her right now, but I will!" Tasha said to herself.

"Give up!" said the sorceress. "You know you have no chance against me!"

"Oh, I am going to get you, witch! You better believe that!" Tasha shouted back as she waited for the perfect opening to attack.

The sorceress then began sending bigger debris Tasha's way. At one point, she used her powers to pick up an enormous boulder, which she threw at Tasha hard and fast.

"That's my opening!" Tasha thought to herself. She grabbed a grenade, pulled the pin, and threw it at the boulder. That caused an explosion that destroyed the massive rock, turning it into dust. She then launched herself into the midst of the dust plume. The sorceress couldn't see what was happening until it was too late. Tasha aimed at the witch's head. The witch tried to counter the oncoming attack, but her attempt was unsuccessful. "I got you now, witch!" The speed at which she encountered the sorceress caused both of them to fly into an abandoned building.

CHAPTER FOURTEEN
Talking Back

"Let's hurry and take this guy out so we can go help Tasha!" Crae Crae shouted. Crae and the others surrounded the necromancer warrior.

"All of you are going to die, right here and right now," the warrior said.

"Yeah, yeah. Whatever," Crae replied. Simultaneously, the team charged the necromancer. At the same time, something strange came out of the warrior's back. It was another arm! "What the heck? Where did that come from?"

Suddenly, another voice came from the necromancer.

"This thing's back is talking!" yelled another team member.

The voice said, "Come out, my legion brothers. It's time for blood!" After saying that, a figure stepped out from the warrior's back.

"Dude! A demon just came out his back! What now?" another team member said with genuine concern.

Crae was unmoved. "This necromancer has demons known as legion—multiple demons that can inhabit a human. There's no telling how many more are still in him. Still, no matter what, we are going to kill them all and help Tasha!"

Then, four more legions came out and rushed towards Crae and the others. The battle for London was quickly intensifying.

"Max out your suits NOW!" Crae yelled.

The legion demons could not figure out why they couldn't hurt the team. "Why can't we hurt you?" they asked.

"Don't worry about that. Just know we can hurt and kill you!" Crae replied. After saying that, he struck one of the demons, killing it instantly. "Hold on, Tasha! We're coming!"

Then, another demon came out.

"They're going to keep coming out of the necromancer!" a team member shouted.

"You're right. We must deal with him first," Crae stated.

An overconfident team member hollered, "I got him!" and went running towards the demon. Crae and the others tried desperately to stop him, but it was too late. The necromancer grabbed the team member and stuck his weapon into his chest, killing him. The team watched helplessly as their friend died right before their eyes.

The necromancer threw the lifeless body at the team. It was the first time they lost anyone since the war began.

"I see demons can't penetrate your suits because they're made from angelic metal, but my weapon can cause deadly harm!" the monster shouted while laughing.

"You're going to pay for that," Crae announced.

"You know you don't stand a chance against me, especially since you have no leader. She's busy fighting my leader."

"You don't know what we're capable of doing. We will kill you and destroy what's in you!"

Crae and the team gathered and prepared for another assault. "Y'all deal with the demons. I'm going to handle him. I don't want another one of those things to exit his body. Once you kill the demons, we will finish him off."

CHAPTER FIFTEEN
The Legion Brothers

Meanwhile, Eion and the demon leader remained in a heated battle.

"I see your friends have met my other legion brothers," the demon taunted.

Eion looked back and saw his team warring with the necromancer. Although confident in their abilities, he knew he must end his fight quickly so he could help the others. "I'm not worried. I have all the faith in the world for my team. They will win," he thought to himself.

CHAPTER SIXTEEN
He Will Rise

Tasha and the sorceress' fight was nearing its end. The sorceress could not understand why her powers weren't working against Tasha.

"Why are my powers not working on you?"

"I know why, witch!" Tasha screamed. She then launched at the sorceress, causing them to fall near where some of the survivors were hiding. "Oh, no. This is not good," Tasha thought to herself. She yelled at the survivors, "Get out of the way—NOW!"

Before they could run, the witch grabbed one of the survivors and put her razor-like fingernails against the throat of her victim. "I'm only going to ask one more time. How is it that you can keep up with me? Tell me now, or I will kill her."

Tasha didn't want to tell her, but she had no choice.

"Our suits are made from angelic metal. Demons and black magic do not work on us. Now you know. Let her go!"

The sorceress said, "Oh. I see. Okay." She then sliced the woman's neck, killing her.

That action instantly enraged Tasha. "I'm going to kill you!"

She charged towards the witch, and they engaged in the most heated battle to date. They went toe-to-toe until Tasha eventually got the upper hand, knocking the sorceress to the ground and then jumping on her, repeatedly punching the witch in the face until she pleaded for mercy.

"Please!" the sorceress begged. "You win. I'll tell you everything you need to know."

Tasha stopped beating her long enough to say, "Speak, witch!" The look of anger on her face and tone of her voice let the sorceress know she was not playing around.

"There are several places in this world that are the darkest on the planet. Why do you think some places are hit harder by our attacks? Those places are where the four largest gates are located and will open soon. One is near the Netherlands. Two are in Africa. The biggest and what is known as the main gate is located in the United States. It is from there where he will rise."

"Who will rise?" asked Tasha.

"He who has many heads. The most powerful is the head of hate, but once all heads are together, our true lord will rise. You know of whom I speak. No matter what you do, you cannot stop what's coming. You cannot stop the unleashing."

As Tasha listened with dismay, she dropped her guard for a second too long, giving the sorceress a chance to make her move. She pulled out a blade and stabbed Tasha in the stomach. The blade was a special kind, enabling it to penetrate her armor.

"I knew it! The only way to penetrate that suit was with another angelic blade. Too bad you won't be able to warn the others. It is here that you will die!"

"No, witch. This is where YOU die!" Tasha quickly pulled out her hidden dagger and thrusted it into the sorceress' chest. As the witch fell to her knees, Tasha said, "Witch, you made me go 95 on you! Anyway, thanks for the information. I will gladly pass it on."

The sorceress then closed her eyes and began speaking a demonic chant. "I just passed on the information as well," she said as a sinister grin spread across her face.

"DIE, WITCH!" Tasha yelled—and then she quickly beheaded her to be sure she was truly dead.

Tasha then fell to the ground, exhausted from her one-on-one battle. "I must tell everyone the sorceress knows about our suits and has spread the word. Get up, Tasha!" Using every bit of strength she had left, she began crawling towards Crae, all while losing blood from her stab wound and trying not to blackout. "God, give me the strength to make it."

CHAPTER SEVENTEEN
Before I Go

Crae glanced over and saw Tasha's badly-wounded body. "Hold on, Tasha! We're coming!" he yelled. Crae then contacted Eion, letting him know Tasha was hurt and that they were trying to reach her.

Eion could feel Tasha's life slipping away.

The demon said to Crae, "I now know your secret. I know the type of metal your suit is made from."

Crae hollered to the others, "Tasha needs us—NOW!"

The demon legion said, "We know how to deal with you all now."

"Shut up! I don't care what you know!" Crae shouted. He and the others put everything they had into fighting the demons and necromancer, finally killing and defeating them all. They suffered injuries in the process, but they were victorious. Crae then ran to Tasha's side. "I'm here, Tasha. I got you."

With a weak voice, Tasha said, "I have the information we came for…"

CHAPTER EIGHTEEN
The Darkest on Earth

Eion's eyes began to glow at the demon as he felt Tasha's and the other team members' lives leaving their bodies.

"You are neither human nor an angel," the demon taunted.

"I told you I have no worries about my team. Your army is defeated," Eion taunted back.

The demon looked around with disappointment. "Well, I'm still going to kill you!"

Before the demon could make a move, Eion went right through it, quickly killing his adversary. He then ran to Tasha and the others. Once there, he immediately grabbed Tasha's hand while Crae called for the medical team. "We need immediate attention! We have multiple team members down! Repeat! We have multiple team members down!"

"We are on the way," came the response from the medical team.

"You hear that, Tasha?" Eion asked. "Hold on, buddy."

"I must tell you what I learned," Tasha said weakly. "The reason why some places were hit harder than others is that those places are the darkest ones on earth. Three big gates are about to open soon. One is in the Netherlands, where Sonya is. The other is in Africa, where Anna is. The main gate is in the States."

"Okay, Tasha. Save your strength. The medical team is almost here," said Eion.

"No. That's not all. They know about the angelic metal. They know how to penetrate our suits. Their mission now is to unleash all the heads to unchain him. You must tell everyone, Eion."

"Okay, Tasha. I will. Stop talking now. Please save your strength." He spoke those words as tears filled his eyes.

"It's okay, guys," she said as she grabbed Eion's and Crae's hands. "I wouldn't change what happened for the world. We are the Ruffnecks. I love every single one of you." As the helicopters began landing, with her last breath, Tasha said one word: "Win."

CHAPTER NINETEEN
Major Losses

The rescue and medic team tended to the wounded and began loading up the surviving refugees, prepared to take them to the ark.

The warriors experienced their first major casualties since the war for humanity started. Eion lost half his team, but their sacrifices weren't for nothing, for they retrieved the information they needed. Although the remaining team members wanted to grieve the loss of their fallen comrades, they knew doing so will have to wait.

Eion contacted the other team leaders to tell them what his team learned, but he couldn't reach those in the States. "Something is blocking my communication."

"Yeah, I know. I'm being blocked, too," Gadin stated with frustration.

"Are you okay, bro?" Anna asked. "I can tell you are hurting. I'm sorry about what happened there."

"Yeah. I'll be okay, sis. Thanks."

"We are all sorry, Eion," said Sonya.

"Eion, soon as you get everyone on the ark, head to Africa where Anna is. I'll go to where Sonya is once I'm done here," Gadin instructed.

"Okay. Y'all be careful."

Gadin said to himself, "I just hope those gates don't open until we get there. Eziah, I know you can feel it coming."

CHAPTER TWENTY
This Is Not A Drill

In South America, Gadin and his team, The Renegades, were in a heavy battle that has gone on for days. They, too, were fighting to save what's left of humanity in that country.

"Gadin, if they know how to get through our angelic armor, that will make our mission much more difficult," said Danny.

"Yes, it will be a challenge, but that's why we must stay focused on the battle, try to save the people, and get out of here alive. Remember that a lot of the demons are fallen angels. They have angelic weaponry, too, and can cut through our defenses. Now that our enemy knows that, things are about to change for the worst. However, we must remain positive. We knew this day would come." As soon as Gadin said that, someone contacted him from the ark, letting him know there's something from above coming in fast, just North of their position. "So, they're finally coming from the skies. Send out the Ace squadron," he commanded.

On the ark, a voice came over the intercom saying, "All Ace fighter pilots: Report to your fighter jets at once. This is not a drill. Repeat. This is not a drill. Ground teams need air support immediately."

All the arks have jets with the best pilots in the world. The warriors knew that attacks would eventually come from the skies, so they prepared themselves for just this moment.

As the pilots scrambled to their jets, the squadron's leader, Captain Toney, told all his pilots, "Okay, guys. Our ground teams need our support, so let's give it to them!" One by one, each jet took off towards the location where Gadin and the rest of the team were waiting.

"We must hold on, team, and hope our air support arrives before they do," said Gadin.

"Gadin, we have hounds coming in…and something else that looks like some type of spider," reported a team member.

"Those are nightcrawlers."

Danny said, "We need to regroup somehow and get ourselves together."

Gadin then punched the ground, causing it to crack. He began lifting the cracked earth in a show of strength, making a wall a mile long, trying to give his team and him time to regroup before making their next move.

"That wall won't hold them long," Nathan said, "and my scanners are detecting them closing in fast from the sky."

"Ace squadron, what's your ETA [estimated time of arrival]?" Gadin yelled.

Captain Toney replied, "ETA is now. We are right on them and about to engage."

One of the other pilots said, "Look at them! They look like a swarm of locusts!"

"Remember your training, squad. Prepare to engage. Here they come! Let them have it!" Toney yelled.

"They're fast!" hollered one of the pilots.

"So are we!" said another.

For a while, it looked like the Ace squadron was winning the battle in the skies, until…

"Guys, I have one on my tail! I can't shake it! I can't shake it!"

"Hold on! We're coming! We're coming!"

Just then, the demon threw something and hit the jet's tail.

"I'm hit! I'm hit! I'm going down!"

"We're coming! Hold on!"

"It's too late, guys. I'm sorry," the pilot said sadly as he watched the demon throw another weapon at him. Once it connected with the jet, it exploded into a million pieces.

"Captain, we just lost one," a pilot reported.

Everyone heard what just happened. Gadin knew things were about to get worse and that they, too, would start losing fighters.

CHAPTER TWENTY-ONE
The Oldest Demons

Gadin felt a very powerful, ominous presence. "Get ready, everyone! They're about to breach the wall!"

When the wall fell, there was something strange waiting on the other side. It was standing tall, staring at the team.

"Oh, my God! What is that?!" asked one of the soldiers.

"A Dominion," replied Gadin. "That's a very powerful demon that was once an angel. It's been a long time since I've seen one of them. I sense nothing but wrath coming from it."

The Dominion stood there, tall as a tree, with its black razor wings. Everyone watched in stunned disbelief as they witnessed one of Hell's purest evils.

The pilots were trying their best to deal with the situation and make it to the ground team. "Gadin, we are trying to reach you, but we are having a hard time fighting these things!" Captain Toney reported.

"Those things are Dominions."

"Oh. Dominions. They are among the oldest of demons. That explains a lot," Toney replied.

"Do what you can, Toney."

"Roger that," he replied. To the pilots, he said, "Guys, you heard Gadin. You now know what they are, so we have to change our strategy."

On the ground, the Dominion looked directly at Gadin with an evil grin. As his grin grew wider, the skies darkened to a night sky.

"This doesn't look good, Gadin," Danny said.

"I know. He's trying to overwhelm us with more demons."

In the sky, Toney told the pilots to turn on their special night-vision lenses. "They think that just because it's getting pitch black, our fighting capabilities will be affected. Well, they got another thing coming!"

CHAPTER TWENTY-TWO
A Legendary Saint

Back on the ground, the demons charged at the team. Gadin told Danny, "Losing is not an option. We will win this and get everyone out of here."

The Dominion stood in place for a while longer before charging at Gadin with a mighty burst. Gadin countered, and they headed straight for each other. As they collided, the force of their impact caused the ground to shake for miles around.

"You are one of the saints. It will be a pleasure killing one of the so-called 'Legendary Saints,'" the Dominion teased.

"You will try...and you will lose," Gadin said with confidence.

CHAPTER TWENTY-THREE
They Keep Coming

Danny and the others continued to battle the hounds and nightcrawlers. "These eight-legged freaks are fast," yelled Danny. He then jumped on one of the nightcrawler's back, which caused the beast to turn its head completely around in an attempt to bite him. "Yo! These jokers can turn their heads around 360 degrees like an owl with no eyes!" Danny quickly beheaded the beast and then asked himself, "If they have no eyes, how can they see?"

"Danny, we are being overwhelmed," shouted Shae.

"I know! I know! We have to keep hitting them hard. We cannot let them win!" He knows they must do something fast to change the outcome, or they will not survive. "There has to be a way to defeat these nightcrawlers," he thought.

Someone radioed in from the ark, saying, "There's a gate nearby. That's why the demons keep coming, no matter how many we kill."

Danny knew they had a serious problem. He can't call for the medical team to help because they would get wiped out as soon as they stepped foot on the ground. He also knows as long as the gate remains open, the situation was going to get much worse. It was then that Danny remembered what Gadin told him:

"Danny, everyone has a gift of some kind. You and Jowel are the most strategic people I know. Y'all are the best at what you do and can devise any plan to get out of anything. I believe in you. We all believe in you. Trust yourself. Most of all, trust in God. He gave you that gift for a reason."

It was then that Danny took a good look at the battlefield and started to figure out some things. Like moles, the nightcrawlers have poor vision and rely on vibrations, sounds, and smells. He asked one of the team members, "Hey! Do you still have a sound grenade?"

"Yeah. Why? You know it won't affect the hounds. In fact, it will only make them meaner!"

"I know, but it's not for them. It's for the nightcrawlers. I think their sense of hearing is more sensitive than the hounds' because their vision is so poor. That's how they're distinguishing who we are. I'm going to throw off their senses."

Once he had the sound grenade in hand, Danny changed the frequency and then threw it. He yelled out, "SOUND BOMB!" When it exploded, it sent a powerful soundwave that caused the nightcrawlers to go into a frenzy, losing their minds and disrupting their senses. They were confused and started to attack the hounds.

"It worked! My ears are ringing, but it worked! That's their weakness. Now is the time to strike back while we have a chance! Use your sound grenades, everyone! Change them to a higher frequency," Danny instructed.

After everyone did what they were told, the battle shifted in their favor. They gained the upper hand by turning the creatures against each other. The Dominion leader watched as his army was being defeated.

"Hmm… Looks like your army is getting wiped out," Gadin mocked. "Great job, Danny," he said to himself. "I knew you would figure it out."

The Dominion looked at Gadin and said with a smile, "Oh, I have many more soldiers." As his eyes turned bright red, hordes of demons spilled out the gate.

"As long as that gate remains open, he's going to keep summoning more and more demons!" Gadin thought to himself.

"What are we going to do?" Nathan asked. "We don't have enough sound grenades, and the demons keep coming!"

"I know! We must close that gate," Danny said. He then contacted Gadin, letting him know they can't reach the gate because there are too many demons.

"Don't give up!" Gadin yelled in response.

CHAPTER TWENTY-FOUR
Firebirds

In the skies, the Ace squadron remained in a furious fight.

"Okay, guys. It looks like we have no choice," said Captain Toney. "We are going to have to turn up the heat so that we can help our guys destroy that gate!"

It was time to initiate 'Operation Firebirds.' This tactic allows each fighter jet to increase its exterior heat by 30% with the use of the angelic metal they are made from. They are the same ones that allow them to raise the temperature and turn into a fiery weapon. Captain Toney knew they could not go past 30% because anything higher than that would disrupt bodily functions due to stress on the body.

The Dominions could not believe what was happening. The jets were faster and super-hot. Their weapons couldn't reach the fighter jets.

Although the Ace squadron gained the upper hand on the situation, the beasts kept coming because of the open gate.

"Hey, Danny. How's it going on closing that gate?" Captain Toney asked. "We won't be able to keep up with firebird mode much longer!"

"I'm working on it. There's just too many of them. We can't get through them to close it!"

Then, out of nowhere, a missile came flying, hitting a Dominion and destroying it. It came from the Eagle squadron —

from Eion and his team's ark out of London! The Ruffnecks joined the battle!

"Hey! What's up, guys? We're here to back y'all up!" said Jesse.

"We sure are glad to see you!" exclaimed Toney.

"Come on now. You can't have all the fun," Jesse teased. She then instructed her squadron to initiate firebird mode.

"You heard what she said! Let's burn them up!" one of the squad members said with joy.

With both squadrons in firebird mode, it gave them a chance to win the air battle.

CHAPTER TWENTY-FIVE
Swiftness and Timeliness

On the ground, Eion and his team ran to meet Danny. "What's the plan, Danny?" Eion asked.

"Eion! I thought you were on the way to Africa!"

"We were, but something told me we needed to come here first, so here we are! So, what do you want us to do? We are here to support you guys, no matter what."

Danny was truly appreciative. "We need to make a way through the demons so that a small group can slip through to plant the spiritual bombs and blow that gate shut. Gadin is busy right now dealing with that other thing."

"I know. I wish I could help him, but I know I'd just get in the way."

"Gadin would want you to help us, anyway," Danny said assuredly. "That thing doesn't stand a chance against Gadin!"

"You're right about that!"

Danny told his team, "The Ruffnecks are going to help make a way so we can close the gate." He then selected two of his team members to accompany him. He knew he must be swift and that the timing must be perfect for the plan to work and to put an end to the battle.

From the air, Jesse said, "Guys, we can't keep this firebird mode up too much longer. How's it going down there?

Some of Captain Toney's pilots have already come out of firebird mode. A few others are still in it but fading."

"She's right, guys," chimed in Captain Toney. "I don't want to put any added pressure on you, but we can't hold out much longer."

Eion replied, "Roger that. We are on it now. Okay, team! Let's make way for Danny and his guys to get through!"

"Yes! Let's get wild! We got y'all!" shouted Crae.

Eion led the attack, making a path as everyone else held the enemy at bay. Danny and the others raced to the gate, running as fast as their suits allowed.

"Let's go! Let's go!" yelled Danny.

CHAPTER TWENTY-SIX
You Don't Want A Piece of This

As Gadin and the Dominion leader's fight was coming to an end, with Gadin severely beating down his opponent, the leader watched as Danny's team made moves toward the gate. It looked at Gadin for a brief moment and then took off running towards the group.

Eion saw the demon coming straight for them and yelled with obvious distress in his voice, "Look out! It's coming right at you!" Eion knew there was no way he could reach his team in time.

Danny looked at the beast coming and screamed, "Just keep running!"

As the Dominion closed in, Gadin caught up just in the nick of time and rammed it, throwing the beast off course and diverting its attention from Danny and the others. "No, you don't! You wanted a piece of me, so we're going to finish this!"

Danny and the others finally reached the gate, set the bombs, and ran clear away from the coming destruction.

Just before the bombs exploded and before Gadin was about to end the Dominion's life once and for all, the Dominion told him, "You will still lose the battle!" Those were the beast's last words as Gadin struck it with a final blow.

At the same time the bombs started going off to close the gate, the Dominion leader fell to the ground. The teams accomplished their goal...or so they thought.

CHAPTER TWENTY-SEVEN
Don't Look Back

"The gate's closed!" Captain Toney shouted. "Let's finish this!" The air and ground battles turned in the warriors' favor, and they started eliminating the remaining demons with ease.

Gadin, however, couldn't help but worry about the Dominion leader.

"Hey, guys. I see black smoke rising from the ground," Jesse said.

"Oh, no. Shadow demons." Gadin's face had a noticeable expression of concern. "Get all the survivors out of here now!" He then called both arks to request immediate evacuation teams.

The black smoke began to consume some of the survivors the teams tried so desperately to protect.

Danny looked at the scene before him in disbelief. "Nooo! We closed the gate! We won the war!"

"Danny! Hey, Danny! Snap out of it! We must get these people out of here!" Eion gently coaxed.

"Guys, you have to get out of there!" yelled Captain Toney. "The ones who are already possessed are becoming night creepers!"

"Toney, we must get them some more time," Jesse pleaded.

"You're right. All pilots: Prepare to launch your missiles. We have to give them more time to save what's left of the survivors!"

Shae yelled, "The evac teams are here!"

"Let's get these people out of here," said Gadin. He and the others tried to rescue those who were not yet consumed by the black smoke that was quickly spreading.

"Keep moving!" Danny shouted as he, Eion, and the others fought to hold off the night creepers. Once the survivors were on board, he asked, "Is that everyone?"

He heard various replies over the radio.

"Yes."

"Roger."

"We're full."

Danny continued. "Okay. When I give the signal, I need both air teams to release the mega bombs and eliminate everything on the ground."

Suddenly, they heard a team member's radio crackle to life. "Danny, we have five people with us, and we're surrounded by the black smoke in a building."

"You need to hurry. In a few minutes, you will all be overtaken by the smoke!" Jesse yelled.

The team member looked at the scared survivors and then said, "These people won't make it. They'll be consumed as soon as they step foot outside. We could give them our suits, though. There are five of them and five of us. They will be protected. Plus, it will give them added speed so that they can run faster. The smoke won't affect us because of our training."

Danny said rather matter-of-factly, "Still, you all will be overtaken before you can reach us. You won't make it."

Almost simultaneously, Eion and Gadin said, "I'm coming."

Just as they spoke those words, another burst of black smoke was released right in front of the group in the building.

"No, don't come," the team member said. "It's too late. You must save the ones who are with you now and the ones on the way out of here. We're giving them our suits now." The team member explained to the survivors that the suits would protect them from the smoke and give them the ability to run fast. "We will hold them off while you all get to safety." As the survivors put on the suits, the team member told Danny, "They are about to exit now."

"Okay, but y'all better be right behind them."

The team member told the survivors, "When I count to three, run—and don't look back. We'll be right behind you. Ready? One…two…three…RUN!" They took off running like lightning streaks through the sky.

"I see them! I see them!" yelled Danny. "Where are you guys?"

"We are here holding off the demons!"

"Come now!" Danny shouted.

"No, Danny. It's too late. Just get them out of here. Tell the teams to fire the missiles now!"

Danny looked at the building the warriors were in with great sadness. He had no choice but to help the last surviving five board the helicopter. He then told the air team to launch the missiles. The pilots hesitated. They did not want to do it.

From the radio, the five warriors all said, "It's okay. Do it now, before it's too late. We can't hold out." The night creepers soon overtook them.

All the pilots then launched the mega bombs, destroying the entire country in the process.

Everyone looked down at the carnage with sadness. From both arks, they saw the country in flames and thought of the loss of their friends who sacrificed their lives for others.

"This wasn't supposed to happen this way," Danny cried. "We lost."

"Danny, if you hadn't figured out how to stop the nightcrawlers and destroy the gate, there would have been no survivors," Gadin said with sincerity. "We are all hurt and saddened by the loss of our dear friends, but we must continue to fight on behalf of them. Now, Sonya and Anna need our help. There are still three colossal gates that will soon open."

Even though Danny knew Gadin was right, he still couldn't help but feel like he wished he could have done more. At the same time, he knows he must remain focused, for the next big battle was on the horizon.

CHAPTER TWENTY-EIGHT
What's Your Position?

Running in the night through a field of grass were Sonya and her team, the Silent Knights. They specialized in recon missions, as well as entering hostile places that were almost completely overrun with demons and a few survivors. Because of their unique training and techniques, they could quickly and quietly rescue others—and close gates. One might say they were like ninjas, unseen and unheard, even to the demons moving in the shadows at night.

The Netherlands is the team's last place and final mission before meeting up with the others on the arks. However, this particular mission is sure to be the hardest for them to complete—and they know it.

"What's everyone's position?" Sonya asked.

"We are about to come up on Giethoorn, where that group of people is hiding," replied MaeLing.

"Okay. Be careful. I'm sensing a lot of negative energy here—more than the other places we've been."

"Roger that. We are already detecting demons in the vicinity," confirmed MaeLing.

"This is our last stop, so we need to get these people out and quickly find the gate, close it, and get out of here as soon as possible. I don't like the feeling I'm getting," Sonya replied. "Contact me once you reach your destination."

"Okay. Over and out."

"We're at Zaanse Schans," replied Shane. "There's also a lot of activity going on here."

"Guys, be careful," Sonya instructed. "Something seems off."

"We'll be okay," both replied.

"Mae, y'all stay safe," Shane said with a voice laden with concern.

"Thanks. Y'all, too," replied MaeLing.

At that, everyone's radio went silent, and each group went on their way to complete their respective mission.

CHAPTER TWENTY-NINE
Uncomfortable Feelings

Ahead, there seems to be a gathering of some sort, but there's a small group of survivors, locked behind the closed doors of a building. As the team walks toward the gathering, negative energy spikes occur repeatedly.

Shane turned to his small team of three—Damen, Felicity, and Yaharey—and said, "We must get those people out of there. Something is about to go down." The four of them made plans to attempt to get past the hundreds of demons to try and save the people who are trapped with the demons closing in on them. "Okay. Let's be fast and quiet while we save them."

Damen took another look and said to himself, "Something's not right."

"The energy keeps increasing every five minutes. If we're going to do this, we better go now," said Felicity.

"Okay. Let's go. Once we reach those windmills, we'll have some cover," replied Shane.

The team then took off running through the darkness of the night.

CHAPTER THIRTY
A Sense of Worry

Sonya was feeling uneasy as the team that was with her finished destroying some demons and rescued a bunch of survivors.

"What's wrong? You look worried," asked an observant team member.

"I am worried."

"The others will be fine, right? I mean, they can handle anything, right?"

"I have no doubt they can, but that's not what's worrying me. It's what I keep sensing."

CHAPTER THIRTY-ONE
Going Unnoticed

When MaeLing and her team reached their destination, she contacted Sonya. "Sonya, we're here. We found the last group of survivors in this area and are going in to get them."

"Okay. Go as quickly as you can."

"What's wrong, Sonya? You've never been like this when we are on a mission."

"I'm worried about Shane and the others. There's strong, negative energy growing in their location."

"Oh. Yeah. We picked up on that as well. We will be as fast as we can and then go to where Shane and the others are." MaeLing and her team moved quickly. They slayed the demons they encountered without being noticed by others.

CHAPTER THIRTY-TWO
Preventing Utter Destruction

Meanwhile, in Zaanse Schans, things were starting to get really serious for Shane and his team. Felicity quietly sent a note to the survivors that were surrounded by the demons, using a bow gun to deliver the message so that the demons wouldn't hear them.

One of the survivors saw it and picked it up. "It's a note."

"What does it say," asked another.

"It says, 'Help is coming. Please stay quiet. No matter what, do not go outside.'"

So, that's just what they did: stayed as quiet as they could.

The team then started making their move toward the survivors. They approached from the rear, where there weren't as many demons. When they safely reached the group inside, one of the people said, "Thank God, you are here."

Shane asked them to remain silent and stay close.

"What's going on? What are those things?" one of them asked.

"Demons," replied Damen, "and there aren't many people left in this country. You are the last ones in this part."

"What?!" replied one of the survivors in a sad, scared voice. "Is this the end of the world?"

"In a manner of speaking, but that's what we are trying to prevent," said Felicity.

"Who are you people?"

"We are just some people trying to save what's left of humanity."

Just then, Yaharey said, "Guys, that energy just spiked big time—and I mean big!"

Damen said, "I'm going to check it out."

"Wait, Damen," Shane instructed.

"Man, you know they won't see me. Plus, we need to know what's happening out there."

"Okay. You're right. Make it quick, though. We need to get these people out of here."

Damen took off, trying to get as close as he could without being seen. Once there, he saw a big gate that was just about to open with someone standing beside it. "This doesn't look right," he whispered into the night air.

In an instant, Felicity showed up at his side. "Shane told me to come and check on you."

"Look at that." Damen directed her eyes to the scene before them.

"Oh, my God! And I bet that's a necromancer standing by the gate. That's a colossal sized gate!"

"We need to go back and tell Shane," Felicity stated.

Upon their return, they shared with Shane what they witnessed.

"That must be why they're gathering here," Shane replied thoughtfully. He immediately contacted Sonya. "Sonya, the colossal gate is here in Zaanse Schans. A necromancer witch is guarding it."

"What??? Do not engage. I repeat. Do not engage. Wait until backup gets there. For now, get away from there."

"Sonya, there's not much time. That gate will open any time now, and we won't have time for anyone to get away. We're going to get the survivors out first and then go back to try and prevent that gate from opening." After saying that, Shane purposely cut off their source of communication. "Okay. Let's get these people to safety and then call the evac team. We will return to do what we do best."

When they were far enough away with the survivors, Shane called the evac team and instructed the group to stay where they were while waiting for the evac team to arrive.

"Are you really going back there?" one of them asked.

"Yep! This is what we do," replied Damen.

Shane and the team then turned and ran back to where the gate was located.

"So, how do you want to play this once we get there?" asked Damen.

"Well, we try out best to prevent that gate from opening," Shane replied matter-of-factly.

At the same time, the warriors raced toward the gate that was surrounded by thousands of demons…and guarded by a necromancer witch.

CHAPTER THIRTY-THREE
Step It Up...Pronto

"MaeLing, how's your mission going?" Sonya asked.

"We're wrapping it up now. The demons seemed to suddenly just take off running away."

"That's because Shane found the colossal gate, and it's about to open. They're all heading to where Shane and the others are going to try to stop the gate from opening."

"Oh, no. We must get these people on the helicopters soon so we can make our way to them."

"Okay. I'm on my way there, too." Sonya then called in the airstrike team from the ark, telling them there's a team on the ground that will need their support. She then said to herself, "It all makes sense. Only one person can block my senses: Azel. But why would she show herself...unless she's trying to do something else other than open that gate. I just hope I'm not too late." Sonya then called MaeLing one more time. "How close are you now?"

"We're about 30 minutes away."

"I believe Azel is there. That's why I felt so weird. If she's there, then something is definitely about to go down besides that gate opening. Get there as fast as you can!"

"Gotcha," replied MaeLing, with a level of urgency that matched Sonya's. She called out to her team. "Step it up, guys! The team needs us pronto!" Together, they ran faster than ever. Mae whispered into the night, "We're coming. Just hold on."

CHAPTER THIRTY-FOUR
Out of the League

Back at Zaanse Schans, Shane, Felicity, Damen, and Yaharey engaged their enemies, destroying as many demons as they could without being noticed. They worked collectively to get to the gate to prevent it from opening—until the demons finally caught on to what was happening and started fighting back.

"It looks like they know about us now," Damen said with light laughter.

"It sure looks that way," Shane confirmed.

The four of them were a four-person army, taking out the demons left and right and getting closer to their goal.

"We're almost there!" shouted Felicity.

"But where is that necromancer?" asked Yaharey. No sooner than the sound 'er' was spoken, the witch appeared right in front of him. Yaharey looked at her with a surprised facial expression.

"ENOUGH!" she yelled, and then struck Yaharey, sending him flying backward until he hit the ground—hard.

One of the demons approached the necromancer. "Azel, it's almost time."

Azel sensed something strange coming. "Sonya..."

"This is not good," Damen said. "Sonya's prediction was correct. The first and most powerful necromancer on the planet, Azel, has surfaced. Look at her pale skin and odd eyes. One is jet black, and the other is pure white."

Felicity ran to Yaharey and asked if he was okay.

"Yeah, I'm okay." He might have said he was okay, but when he stood, he was spitting out blood.

"No, you're not," Felicity corrected.

Shane and Damen ran to them. "Hey, are y'all alright?"

"Yes, guys," replied Yaharey.

"We must stop her or at least try to slow her down," Shane stated.

"That is Azel, Shane. We are out of our league here," Damen said with a loud sigh.

"I know, but we have to at least try until Sonya and the others make it."

CHAPTER THIRTY-FIVE
Changing Course

Meanwhile, Sonya was racing her way to the other team when she was contacted by Gadin. "Sonya, are you there?"

"Yes."

"I've been trying to contact you for the past few days."

"It's Azel, Gadin. She's been blocking us so nobody would detect her presence."

"That explains why we couldn't reach the others. That witch has been blocking us with her black magic this whole time. Sonya, there are four major gates: One where you are, two others in Africa where Anna is, and one in the U.S."

"I know. That's where I'm heading now. My team found it and is trying to stop it from opening. I'm feeling something else, though," Sonya said.

"Well, I'm on my way to you. I'm going to tell Eion to head to Africa to help Anna." Gadin then called Eion. "Is your team ready?"

"Yes, we're ready."

"Good. Head straight to Africa. Your sister is going to need your help."

In an instant, Eion and his team changed course and headed toward Africa.

CHAPTER THIRTY-SIX
Feel the Rage

In Zaanse Schans, the team continued to fight Azel and the other demons, just to buy some time. However, with Azel being as powerful as she was, she kept overwhelming them. Despite being badly wounded, the warriors kept fighting.

"It's useless to resist! You are outnumbered and outmatched. You will never defeat me!" Azel taunted while laughing hysterically.

Breathing hard, Felicity replied, "Wait for it, witch."

"Wait for what?"

Just then, Sonya arrived, striking Azel and sending her into one of the windmills.

"For THAT!" Damen yelled.

With just a moment to spare, Sonya asked the team if they were all okay.

"We're just glad you are here," said Yaharey.

"Yeah! That witch was kicking our tail!" agreed Shane.

Felicity asked the question everyone wanted the answer to: "Is she dead?"

"Unfortunately, no. Get ready," Sonya instructed.

Azel rose from the ruins of the fallen windmill. "Well, hello, Sonya. How long has it been?" Her sinister smile was way too creepy.

"You finally showed yourself," came Sonya's reply.

"Well, you are a little late."

"It's not going to work, Azel."

"Oh, but wait for it!"

The gate began to open. Something walked out of it. Each member of the team had eyes that bulged with fear. Sonya turned towards them and yelled, "RUN! NOW!" The creature then charged toward Sonya, seething with rage.

"Look out!" shouted Yaharey to Sonya.

The creature caught her off guard, grabbed her, and rammed her body into a building.

"Feel the rage! Feel the wrath!" Azel taunted merrily. She summoned the demon called 'Wrath,' which was one of the devil's heads.

Sonya found the strength to kick the creature away so that she could gather herself for a quick moment.

"We still gotta close that gate!" Shane yelled.

"But how?" Damen asked. "That witch is not going to let us get close enough!"

Suddenly, a commotion drew everyone's attention to the sky. MaeLing and the team arrived, along with aerial support.

"I will not let any of you interfere!" screamed Azel.

"This is our chance, while she's distracted," Yaharey said.

"You need to chill," Felicity advised. "You are severely injured."

"I don't care about that. We need everyone if we are going to have a chance to close that gate and prevent anything else like that thing from coming out!"

"Okay, buddy. We understand," replied Damen.

All the while, Sonya kept going back and forth with the demon called 'Wrath.' Then, Gadin showed up and landed a vehicle on the demon.

"Are you okay?" Gadin asked Sonya.

"Yeah, but what you did is not going to stop it. Azel summoned that thing."

"What?! No way!"

"Get ready, Gadin. It's about to come out!" Just then, the demon busted out of the flames and charged toward them. "We must stop her before she summons another head!"

CHAPTER THIRTY-SEVEN
Distracted...For Just A Moment

Disappointingly, the others were having difficulties trying to reach the gate, even those flying the fighter jets. Azel destroyed every missile that got close to the gate, and then she began destroying the jets.

"She's blocking everything we throw at the gate! She's picking us apart!" MaeLing said and then contacted Shane. "We're going to try and come at the witch from all sides to distract her long enough for y'all to reach the gate."

"Okay. We got this!" he replied.

Felicity said, "They won't be able to keep her distracted for more than a few minutes."

"Well, let's make those few minutes count!" Gadin then told Sonya, "We can't let them face her. They'll get slaughtered! I'll handle this while you go help the others."

"Are you sure?"

"Yes. Go quickly."

Sonya ran off to help her team, but 'Wrath' tried to stop her from leaving. Gadin grabbed him. "No, you don't! Your fight is with me now!" Then they began to battle.

CHAPTER THIRTY-EIGHT
Nowhere Is Safe

Sonya contacted her team. "Let me deal with Azel. All of you focus on destroying the gate before anything else comes out."

Azel turned around and saw Sonya coming towards her and 'Wrath' battling Gadin. "I see the others have come to help. No matter what, you will still lose."

"Shut your mouth!" Sonya repeatedly tried to strike Azel with her sword, but each swing was blocked by her evil powers.

MaeLing yelled to Shane, "This is our chance! We'll deal with the demons. Y'all go the gate. Air team, make a way for them!"

"Understood," replied one of the pilots.

"Let's go!" Shane shouted.

As the four of them made their way towards the gate, Azel caught sight of them approaching and getting too close. "No, you don't!" Right then, her white eye turned completely black. Instantly, more demons burst from the ground and attacked the small group.

"Are you kidding me? What are these things? Zombies?" asked Damen.

"I don't know," Felicity replied. "With that witch, anything is possible."

"Yaharey, keep going. Close that gate!" yelled Shane. "We can handle this."

Yaharey nodded his understanding and kept moving, still severely wounded and coughing up more blood. Azel saw him and started sending flying spikes his way.

"Watch out!" screamed Shane.

Multiple spikes struck Yaharey, but he kept going. The warriors watched as their friend gave his all to close the gate.

Then, spikes started hitting Shane and the others.

"No!" yelled Sonya!

Yaharey fell to the ground. "Hold on!" screamed MaeLing. Yaharey kept crawling towards the gate. When he was close enough, he stood, pulled out the bomb, and blew up the gate, destroying it from the inside. MaeLing caught him before he hit the ground. The force from the explosion exiting the hole caused everyone to go flying backward. Even the fighter jets temporarily lost control due to the blast.

"Stay with me, Yaharey," MaeLing cried while holding him tightly.

"Where are the others?" he asked weakly.

MaeLing looked around. She saw some of the team trying to get up and get themselves together after being blown to the ground. Shane, Damen, and Felicity laid motionless with spikes protruding from them. She shook her head as she looked down at Yaharey and said, "It looks like they didn't make it."

Sonya and Gadin got up and asked if everyone was okay, until Sonya saw the three warriors laying there, obviously deceased.

"Where are Azel and that thing?" Gadin asked.

As if in response, the ground began to shake. All around them, anything that remained standing fell to pieces. Azel and 'Wrath' rose from the ground. "I will kill you all!" screamed Azel. She looked directly at Sonya and said through clenched teeth, "You still lose. There's nowhere safe, not even the safe zone." In her most boisterous voice, she then screamed, "UNLEASH THEM!"

CHAPTER THIRTY-NINE
The Death Stare

Gadin turned to Sonya and said, "Tell everyone to get out of here now!"

"You heard him! Everyone fall back! Leave this country immediately!" she instructed.

MaeLing and a few others helped carry Yaharey. Just as Azel and 'Wrath' prepared to attack the retreating, small army again, Gadin put up a spirit wall that saved his people from more harm.

"Ha! That's clever, but it won't hold me back forever!" Azel jeered.

"It will hold you back long enough!" Gadin replied.

Azel then directed her attention to Sonya. "Too bad about your fallen comrades."

Sonya was just about to charge Azel, but Gadin stopped her. "There's nothing we can do for them. We have to get out of here, or we will all die. There will be another time. We will get her. I promise. Right now, we must get everyone out of this country."

The evac helicopters came and picked up the remaining team and other survivors.

After ensuring everyone boarded the transports safely, Gadin said, "Sonya, let's go."

Sonya stood in place a while longer, looking at her fallen teammates before giving Azel a death stare.

"Sonya, we must leave. Anna and Eion need us in Africa." Gadin spoke in a gentle tone with a hint of urgency.

Azel stared back at Sonya as an evil grin spread across her face.

"I will get you," Sonya said with serious resolve. She and Gadin jumped into the helicopter that awaited their entry. As they flew away, Sonya continued to stare at Azel until she was out of sight. She then went over to Yaharey and pleaded with him, "Stay with us."

"Is the gate closed?" he asked.

"Yes," Sonya replied sadly.

"Shane. Damen. Felicity. They didn't make it, did they?"

"No. I'm sorry."

He looked at her as a tear rolled down his cheek. "Oh. Okay." Those were his last words before he died in her arms.

CHAPTER FORTY
A Changing Landscape

Once the team and survivors were on the ark and out of harm's way, they could see the country's entire landscape turn jet black.

Sonya and Gadin had a conversation about the events of the day.

"I know how you feel," Gadin said. "I lost a lot of good people, too."

"Azel summoned 'Wrath'—one of the devil's heads. When she gets the others and summons the devil's head of 'Hate,' you know what that means. What else did she unleash, though?"

"I don't know. I hope Eion reaches Anna in time."

CHAPTER FORTY-ONE
There Are Three

Back in Zaanse Schans, Azel told 'Wrath,' "They have no idea what's coming for them."

A demon then approached them and said, "There are three humans still alive, but barely."

"Really? Show me," Azel demanded. As she walked up to them, she saw it was Shane, Damen, and Felicity. "Interesting…"

"Do you want me to finish them off?" asked the demon.

"No. I have plans for them. Soon, I will gather the rest."

CHAPTER FORTY-TWO
Go, Betsy! Go!

Riding through Tanzania in the Eastern part of Africa was a rugged team led by Anna called 'The Dirt Road Boys.' They were the largest team out of all the rest because they specialized in rugged and large terrains and urban areas. They dealt with larger countries, such as Asia and now, Africa. The team's presence spreads across all of Africa—East, West, North, South, and Central.

The Dirt Road Boys are soon to face their biggest battle since the war for humanity began.

"Hey, these bow-legged hounds are on us like a coon dog on a boar!" Country said.

"Well, step on it, Country!" yelled Patrick.

"I got Betsy going as fast as she can go!"

"Tell Betsy to put some fire in her so we can put some distance between us and those things!"

Someone else chimed in. "There's a dust storm heading our way."

"That ain't a dust storm. That's our girl running toward us like a coyote chasing a roadrunner," Country replied with a smile.

As soon as he finished his countryfied sentence, Anna ran past them and took out the horde of hounds. When she finished that task, she ran and caught up with the fast-moving vehicle, jumping onto the back of the truck. The survivors looked at her, speechless.

"Yeah, I know. Pretty awesome, right?" asked Patrick.

"Listen, there's a whole lot more hounds and crawlers here," Anna stated.

"I know. Do you think it's here?" Patrick looked around, expecting to see it.

"Without a doubt, the Alpha is here somewhere. We need to get back to the camp with our riders. It's getting dark, and the night creepers will soon be roaming. Hey, Country! Let's kick up some dust while we still have light!" Anna joked.

"I gotcha, buddy!"

CHAPTER FORTY-THREE
The Ocean Speaks

Anna then contacted the ark. "Hey, Admiral! How are things going from the sea?"

"Things are going pretty good so far, Anna. No activity out here as of yet, but that worries me."

"Why?"

"Well, if you been at sea as long as I have, you tend to pick up a special sense—like the ocean talks to you, telling you things like it's either going to be smooth sailing or you better tighten up your sails. I've never been wrong."

"That's why you're the Admiral! Have the mako team on alert."

"Already on it," he replied.

"Good deal! I'll check in later. Over and out!"

"Okay, Anna. Over and out!" He then spoke to the ark's crew. "Keep all radar ranges wide and deep as possible. Steady as she goes. We don't want to get caught off guard."

CHAPTER FORTY-FOUR
A Familiar Feeling

As the team got closer to the camp, Anna suddenly felt a familiar feeling. She quickly turned around. "What was that feeling just now?" Anna asked in a curious voice to no one in particular.

"Are you okay?" Patrick asked. "Do you see something?"

"Yeah. I'm okay. I just felt something I hadn't experienced in a long time. Maybe I'm just jumpy."

"I know the feeling. We're all jumpy these days, especially with the Alpha possibly in the area."

Anna continued to look in the direction of that feeling she had. As they continued on their journey to the camp, she kept asking herself, "What was that? Was it me sensing the Alpha? Whatever it was, it was powerful."

CHAPTER FORTY-FIVE
The Flames and the Hounds

In Johannesburg, South Africa, there's another team led by Captain Kemaah. They've been helping wounded survivors and trying to clear the area so that they can get the survivors to safety.

"Yo, we need to put a perimeter around us. At least 20 miles. That should give us some elbow room and time to tend to the wounded. We need to give everyone some food and water before the next attack," Kemaah stated.

"Okay. We're on it," replied Kane. "You heard him. Let's do this quickly."

As the small squad set the perimeter, others tended to the wounded and gave out food and water. Kemaah was going over plans with some of the others, trying to figure out the safest route to get to the rendezvous spot.

"Kemaah, didn't Anna say the Alpha may be here somewhere?" asked Chidike.

"Yeah, that's correct. But no one has seen it. That doesn't mean it's not around. It likely explains why we have been fighting more hounds and crawlers. Think about it. Africa is the perfect environment. Just look at its surroundings. Although I have never seen the Alpha, from what I heard, it's three times the size of the hounds and extremely strong."

"What if we come face to face with it?" asked Chidike.

"We cross that bridge…if we come to it. Right now, we need to focus on what's in front of us and these people we're protecting. The fire that suddenly appeared in the distance is getting closer. As soon as we finish here, we are leaving. I don't like staying in one place for too long."

"I understand," Chidike said. "I'll go check on the others' progress now."

As Chidike walked away, Kemaah kept looking at the fire that was burning miles away. He said to himself, "It looks like it's just burning in one place, almost like it's waiting for something." He then contacted Kane. "How's the perimeter going? You see that fire is still burning out there."

"Yeah, we saw that when we got here. We'll be done soon."

"Okay. Hurry back, Kane. That fire has me bothered."

"Gotcha." Kane then spoke to the men with him. "Guys, let's pick it up. Kemaah wants us back as soon as possible. He's worried about that fire."

"But that fire is miles away," said Cole.

"It doesn't matter. Let's get this done so we can go."

"Guys, I'm picking up multiple readings 60 miles away heading this way," Nuo stated.

Kane quickly sent out the bird that was actually a fast drone, able to cover great distances in a matter of minutes. When the bird reached the location, its camera showed what was coming. "Yep. Hounds. Thousands of them."

"How long before they reach us?" Cole asked.

"At the rate they're going, they'll be here in a couple of hours," Nuo replied.

Kane's impatience grew. "Where are we with the perimeter?"

"Done!" said one of the team members.

"Good. Let's get packed up and get out of here. I'm going to contact Kemaah and tell him about the situation with those hounds. The perimeter is not going to hold them back too long. "Kemaah, thousands of hounds are heading this way. We have about a couple of hours at best before they reach the perimeter, but it won't hold them off for long."

"That means we have an hour to be gone and try to stay ahead of them," Kemaah replied thoughtfully. "Okay, Kane. Get your tails back here fast."

"We're already on our way."

Kemaah ran and told Chidike to tell everyone to load up quickly because the hounds were heading their way. "There's a lot of them. Thousands. We have an hour to get out of here."

Chidike did as he was told, and they worked together to load the people into the truck and pack up all the equipment.

Kemaah turned his attention back to the fire and noticed it started to spread rapidly—right towards them. Kane and the others saw the same thing.

"Hey, that fire wasn't that close before," said Nuo.

"It's spreading and coming right at us," Kane stated.

Cole was obviously frightened by the sight. "If that fire catches up with us, we're going to be stuck between it and those hounds!"

When they finally reached the camp, Kemaah yelled, "Let's go! We gotta go now!" He explained to the group that it was not a coincidence that the fire was waiting for those hounds. "As soon as they started to come was when it began to spread. We have a small window if we head West. Hopefully, we can catch up to the others who are in the central part of the country before that fire cuts us off."

The group quickly left the area, leaving some of the equipment behind.

"The hounds are almost at the perimeter," Nuo said.

Kane spoke with more confidence than he truly felt. "It should keep them at bay long enough to give us time to reach the others."

Kemaah noticed the fire was burning and spreading even faster.

"How is that happening, Kemaah? There's no wind!" exclaimed Kane.

"I know. If we can't get past that fire, we are in trouble. We will have to deal with both the fire and the hounds."

"Then what?" asked Kane. "You know that's no ordinary fire."

"Yeah, I know. It is something else. If we can't make it, we're going to have to face it. With everyone spread across the country, there's no telling how long it will be before anyone can come to our aid — or even if they will be able to."

As Kemaah's team faces the oncoming danger, the other teams in different parts of Africa were also about to soon face dangers themselves.

CHAPTER FORTY-SIX
New Friends

The team in Central Africa were making their way out of Angola into the rainforest of the Congo jungle with their team leader, Dakini, leading the way. "Ryan, what's the visual from the bird drones?" she asked.

"Nothing, really. There are some gorillas. That's about it."

"They're probably scared about what's going on," said Mizzy.

"I wouldn't doubt it," Bai said, "but then again, they may be hostile toward us. To them, man has always been a monster. That's why they had to be protected. They were being killed or captured to be held in captivity. Let's not forget man has been trying to destroy the forest for money."

"I just don't get why some people like destroying this God-given earth and all of its beauty," Mizzy said with a sigh.

"Greed and envy," Dakini replied. "Both play a big role. It's never enough. They always want more and want to control and rule over everything, no matter what or who they hurt or kill in the process. The love of money is the root of all evil."

Ryan gave his two cents. "They don't care, as long as they get what they want."

Mizzy felt the need to change the conversation. "I sure do hope we find some survivors when we reach the city."

"Well, we're about to find some gorillas because they are on the move and heading right towards us!" Ryan yelled.

"Hmm… We must be in their territory," Dakini mused.

As the team got deeper into the jungle, they found themselves surrounded by the gorillas.

"Uh… What are supposed to do now?" Ryan asked, scared out of his mind.

Little by little, the gorillas began coming out of the forest to face the team.

"Everyone stand down. Lower your weapons and do not make any sudden moves. We don't want them to think we are a threat to them," Dakini instructed.

Seemingly out of nowhere, the leader of the gorillas — a large silverback — charged at Ryan.

"Ryan, don't look straight at him!" hollered Dakini.

"Too late," he replied.

"He's showing his strength and dominance to test you. He wants to see how you will react."

"I'm looking down with my eyes closed now, so I'm definitely not looking directly at him."

Then, a baby gorilla burst through the tree line and ran straight to Mizzy. Not thinking about what Dakini said, she moved to try and get out of the way.

"Mizzy, don't move!" yelled Bari.

The silverback saw her move, ran over to her, got in her face, and roared.

Dakini and the others had their weapons at the ready but didn't want to hurt any of the beasts because they all knew they were simply protecting their own. Although Mizzy was visibly shaking, she managed to shift her eyes toward Dakini, giving her a look that said, "It's okay. Stand down."

The silverback then looked at Mizzy and the others as if he knew who they were and knew they wouldn't hurt his family. He then let out another roar. The baby gorilla returned to Mizzy and climbed into her arms.

"I don't know what you did, but whatever it was, it worked. It seems like they like us now," Bai stated with a smile.

"I didn't do anything," Mizzy replied. "It just seems like…"

"It just seems like they knew who we were and that we were coming." Dakini finished what Mizzy was trying to say.

"Do you think Eziah had anything to do with this?" Ryan asked. "You know what he can do, after all."

"True," agreed Dakini, "but I've never known him to communicate with animals, though."

Mizzy let out a sigh of relief, all while continuing to hold the baby gorilla in her arms.

"Let's continue to the city," Dakini said.

As they continued on their journey, the gorillas followed them. "It looks like we have some new recruits. The more, the merrier, I say," Ryan said with glee.

"No. I think they are protecting us," Bari replied.

The team traveled for hours through the thick jungle. Dakini could tell everyone was getting tired and hungry. "Let's rest for a bit. I think we all need to catch our breath and get something to eat. We don't want to be too tired when we reach the city. There's no telling what we'll get into. Besides, it's dark now. We'll get up early and head out."

The group sat down and rested up. Even some of the gorillas sat with them. The younger ones gathered around Mizzy, and she played with them. Some of the others just watched, as if they were on guard.

Ryan stood and announced, "I'm going to climb this tree to get a better view."

As the darkness of night came, everything around them looked both scary and wonderful at the same time. "Wow, listen to that. Everything sounds so alive," Mizzy said. "Look how peaceful the gorillas are. Even if the baby isn't theirs, they still take care of it and guard them like they were their own."

Bari shook his head in agreement. "Yeah, that's why we are trying to protect life itself. If evil wins, none of this will exist anymore."

Ryan remained in the tree, looking around to make sure nothing snuck up on them. Before too long, the silverback climbed the same tree and sat on a thick branch next to Ryan, which caused a look of surprise. He spoke to the gorilla as if he would get a reply. "Oh. I see. You just want to sit and be on the lookout with me." The silverback looked at Ryan and then out into the forest.

A team member approached Dakini and said, "This type of thing does not happen. The others will never believe we chilled with a family of gorillas. This is unbelievable!"

"You're right. They probably won't. This is something meant for only us to witness. It's important that we remember this day."

As the hours in the night grew, so did the danger.

Mizzy drifted off to sleep, and the tree branches started to move towards her like a snake. Ryan and the silverback were still in the tree on the lookout. The gorilla saw the thing moving towards Mizzy and suddenly jumped down to the forest's floor. Ryan wondered what he saw, so he jumped down and ran behind the gorilla. Mizzy slowly opened her eyes in time to see the "branch" about to stick her. The silverback grabbed the branch right before it could stab her, and they roared loudly to warn everyone.

Ryan saw what happened and was like, "What the heck?!"

All the gorillas jumped up and down, roaring in chorus with the silverback.

"What's going on?" yelled Dakini.

"A branch was moving and was about to stab me, and the silverback saved me," Mizzy said with a bit of tremble in her voice.

"We're under attack!" Ryan yelled. "We're under attack!"

"How?" asked Bari. "We never picked up any enemy movement."

"That's because the trees are the enemy. They're moving!" Ryan yelled louder.

The tree branches started attacking everyone in the group.

"We now have enemy movement coming from under the ground!" Ryan screamed.

"It's the nightcrawlers!" yelled Dakini.

The gorillas started fighting the nightcrawlers while the team was trying to deal with the tree branches.

"What the heck is going on?" Mizzy cried.

Bari then lit a flame torch to help fight off the branches.

Dakini hollered, "We must pull out now and try to make it to the city. We're just a few miles away. Let's go!"

The team tried hard to escape the attack, with the gorillas following right behind them. Then, something unseen started to snatch the team members as they were trying to escape.

"Whatever it is, we can't see it. It's blending with the surroundings, so we can't detect what it is!" yelled Mizzy.

Something tried to grab Dakini, but one of the gorillas stepped in and saved her. It was then the being was revealed.

"An elemental," Dakini said to herself. She then shouted, "It's an elemental! That's why we were unable to detect it! Elementals are kinetic beings that can manipulate the elements."

"Oh, great," Ryan said. "Now, we have to deal with those and the crawlers."

"All we gotta do is focus on this elemental. The gorillas are fighting the nightcrawlers," Bari said.

"But how can we even find it if it keeps blending in, especially if its ability is wood?" asked Mizzy.

"We must figure out something fast before it takes us all out," Dakini said.

CHAPTER FORTY-SEVEN
Distress Signal

Kemaah and his team were still trying to outrun the fire and the hounds. Their only window and chance to escape was about to close.

"I'm going to try and contact the team in Central Africa," Kemaah told the group. "Hey, Central team! Can you hear me? We need help ASAP!"

"Kemaah? Is that you?" replied Dakini.

"YES! We are in serious trouble! There's a fire that's trying to cut us off from reaching you, and there are hounds hot on our tail!"

"We can't get to you right now, Kemaah. We are trapped in the congo battling an elemental and crawlers!" She then screamed to her team, "LOOK OUT!"

Kemaah then lost the signal. "Dakini! Dakini!" he yelled into the radio. All he heard was static.

"What's going on?" asked Cole.

"They are also under attack. They can't come," replied Kemaah with obvious distress.

"Our window is gone," reported Nuo. "The fire has completely blocked us, and we can't go through it with these people on the back of these trucks. Our suits will protect us, but they have no protection. Plus, the hounds have broken through the perimeter and are heading our way."

Kemaah fell silent and went into deep thought. Kane noticed the change and asked, "What's up, Kemaah?"

"I'm just thinking about what Dakini said right before we got cut off." He turned and looked at the fire again. "She said they are fighting an elemental right now. It all makes sense why the fire has been acting that way. It's an elemental."

Suddenly, a figure walked out of the fire, fully engulfed in flames.

"It looks like we're about to fight one, as well," said Cole.

"Chidike, can you contact anyone else?" Kemaah asked.

"No. The heat must have fried our communication. I think I can at least send out a distress signal, though."

"Good. Do what you can while we try to deal with this elemental and the hounds." Kemaah then shouted to the others, "Our priority is still these people. That has not changed. Is that clear, everyone?"

Before anyone could respond, a burst of flames came shooting out, right at the convoy.

"EVERYONE GET DOWN!" yelled Cole.

"The hounds are closing in!" shouted Nuo.

Kane jumped into the conversation. "How much ammo do we have left?"

"Not enough!" replied Nuo.

The elemental drew nearer and nearer.

"It's getting closer, y'all!" yelled Kane in a worried voice.

Kemaah needed to get his team in order. They were falling apart. "Okay. Listen. Cole, you, me, and a few others must try to find something to extinguish the elemental. Kane, you and the others do your best against the hounds."

As Kemaah and half of the team went to take on the fiery elemental, the others loaded up their gear to prepare to engage the horde of hounds.

CHAPTER FORTY-EIGHT
It's A Trap

In the Eastern part of Africa, Anna and her team arrived at a temporary safety camp for survivors. It is there the refugees stay until the med and evac teams can come to get them.

Anna began to feel evil danger spreading rapidly. "I can feel the teams. They are in trouble," she said to herself.

"Anna!" called out on the of teammates.

"What is it?"

"There's a distress signal coming from the South team."

"I'm going to them now," Anna replied.

"Wait, Anna. There's another signal coming from the Central team."

The captain from the ark contacted Anna. "Anna, we are getting multiple signals from all the teams. They are all under heavy attack against something they've never faced before."

The teammate added, "Elementals are attacking them."

"Oh, no. Elementals," Anna repeated as worry washed over her face.

"What are you going to do?" asked Amaka. "I know you are strong, but you can't be everywhere at once."

Anna radioed the Admiral. "How long will it take for the other evac team to arrive to pick up the other survivors?"

"Not long. They're headed your way now."

"Good. We need to get these people out of here as quickly as possible while we are not under attack. Tell the rest of the evac teams to head to where the other teams are."

"Okay," replied the Admiral. "Do you want us to send the other team out as well?"

"No. Not yet, but have them on standby. This was all planned to have us distracted from our mission."

Country rushed over to Anna. "Anna, there are two convoys carrying survivors that wrecked a few miles away. The hounds and crawlers are closing in. We won't have time to head out there to save them."

"Lower the defenses, Country. I'm headed out there now."

"But Anna…" Before Patrick could finish, Anna stopped him.

"You know I'm not going to leave them there to be killed!"

"I'm just saying," Patrick continued, "you know it's a trap."

"Then, so be it. I will never forgive myself if those people die, knowing there was something I could've done."

"We have your back, Anna," Country said as he readied his weapons.

"Then, let's go get those people!" Patrick grabbed his weapons, prepared to take the fight to the beasts.

"Let's go! We have no time to waste!" Anna replied.

Anna and a few of her teammates headed out to rescue the survivors involved in the wreck before it was too late. She managed to stay slightly ahead of the others with her speed because she was determined to reach their destination quickly.

CHAPTER FORTY-NINE
The Demon-Human

While the Central and South teams battled wood and fire elementals, the North and West teams were battling earth and wind elementals.

"This is crazy! We are fighting something our weapons cannot even touch! We can handle dark spirits with what we have, but there's nothing in our arsenal to deal with this. Air is something that can cause hurricanes!" Zenny said.

"Yes, we do. We were all provided with weapons to handle these types of situations," replied Chibuzo. "We just have to figure out what they are so that we can neutralize them."

"How?" asked Osumara. "Our weapons go right through him!"

"William, do you have anything yet? It seems like everyone is fighting some kind of element with no way to stop them. You are our best chance to beat them because of your knowledge of the ecosystem," Chibuzo stated.

"I'm trying," William replied. "I just need a little more time."

"Well, buddy, I hate to be the bearer of bad news, but time isn't really on our side," Zenny said with urgency. "The winds are getting stronger by the minute. Soon, these people we came to rescue will be blown away, right along with us!"

"Wait. What did you just say?" asked William.

"What? About all of us being blown away?"

"No. Before that."

"I said the winds are getting stronger by the minute."

"Yes! That's it!" William said excitedly. "I've been timing the wind's velocity and see it gets stronger about every five minutes. He must be expending a lot of energy to make that increase, so he's getting his energy from the air around us. If I'm correct, that means he has to stop, even if it's just for a few minutes, to absorb more air so that he can increase the winds. By doing so, he's revealing his true form!"

"I get it!" Osumara's excitement matched William's. "In his true form, he may be vulnerable!"

"Exactly!" William replied. "That's only if my theory is correct, though. We would have to get close to him to see if that's the case."

Zenny's shoulders slumped. "I knew you were going to say that."

"Okay. We have to figure out how to get close enough to him without being blown to kingdom come," Chibuzo stated. He then instructed one of the other teammates to contact the other teams to let them know the situation. "Tell them we are close to figuring out how to defeat the elements." He looked around and noticed Osumara was gone. "Hey! Where is Osumara?"

"I don't know," Zenny replied. "He was just here."

"Oh, no. He's gone out there," Chibuzo said, pointing towards the air beast.

Osumara struggled to get as close as he could to see if William's theory was correct, and it was. The creature showed its true form for a couple of minutes between each blast of wind. "It's human," he whispered to himself. He hurried back and told the team, "It shows its true form for about two minutes—and check this out: It's not a demon. It's human!"

CHAPTER FIFTY
They Can't Help

As the North team made its plans to defeat the elementals, the West team dealt with the earth elemental and made a discovery while battling it.

"Man, this thing keeps turning from diamond to stone to metal, and it's really getting on my nerves!" Chrissy said in frustration.

"Mine, too," agreed Comfort. "Why hasn't it caused an earthquake to come and swallow us up?"

"Well, team leader, don't you think that's a good thing?" asked Nahara.

"Yeah, but there's a reason, and we need to find out—unless…" Comfort paused. "I'm going to go talk to it."

"You're going to do what?!" Vincent asked with surprise.

"You heard me. Look, the North team is getting close to a solution on how to defeat these things, so we need to buy as much time as we can. Besides, this one hasn't killed any of us this entire time. It could have easily wiped us out all at once. I'm thinking it doesn't really want to kill us, so I'm going to at least try to talk to it."

Vincent jumped out of his seat. "I'm going with you."

As Comfort and Vincent approached the element being, Comfort lowered her weapon and said, "I want to talk to you.

I know you don't want to kill any of us because if you did, you would have done so a long time ago."

In response, the earth element sent a bunch of stones towards them. Right before they were about to strike, the stones stopped, fell to the ground, went down into the dirt, and then began to take shape in human form. Comfort and Vincent could not believe their eyes!

"You...you...you are human?!" Vincent stammered. "And a female?"

The being spoke. "No. I do not want to kill anyone, but the witch is in my head. I've been fighting her as hard as I can, but I can't last much longer. The others are already too far gone, so you must destroy me now while you can. I can feel her taking control. Please, hurry!"

"How can we help you?" asked Comfort.

"You can't," said the earth elemental. "My brothers, sisters, and I are too far gone. Once we surrendered to her, she promised she would help us save the planet. As time went on, we figured out she lied to us. It was too late, though. We were under her total control. The longer we live, the more our soul and heart become darker, to the point we can't even sense each other anymore. I knew right then it was over. I fought as long as I could, but time is running out. That's why you must destroy me before it's too late."

"There has to be something we can do," pleaded Comfort.

"No. There's not. I can't even remember my name or my parents' and siblings' names. I'm begging you. Please. You must destroy me now! I don't want to live like this anymore."

Vincent turned to Comfort and asked, "What should we do?"

Comfort looked Vincent in his eyes and said, "We will do what needs to be done."

Just then, the earth elemental yelled, "Oh, no! I feel myself disappearing. Promise me you will do what needs to be done, please?"

"We promise," replied Comfort.

The duo watched as a tear rolled down the earth elemental's cheek. In an instant, she became pure evil and started her attack strategy again, this time with the purpose of killing everyone in sight.

"Watch out!" Vincent yelled.

"Let's hurry and get back to the others. Hopefully, William has a plan," Comfort said wearily.

CHAPTER FIFTY-ONE
All the Faith

In the East, Anna was the first to arrive at the wreckage. She assured the survivors, "It's going to be okay," as she worked to free them.

Patrick, not too far behind Anna, hollered, "Anna! Some hounds are closing in on you fast!"

Anna turned around and began destroying the few hounds that showed up. As the rest of the team arrived and helped the survivors, Anna asked one of them, "Hey! Where's the other convoy?"

"They are a few miles back."

"Okay. You guys stay here and work on freeing them. I'll be back." Anna made her way to the other convoy, decimating the hounds and crawlers that dared to get in her way.

Patrick called out, "Anna, something big is coming from behind us—and it's fast!"

Country turned around and started shooting at it, hitting it with everything he had. "It's not slowing down!" he yelled.

"It's the Alpha!" shouted Patrick.

Anna's eyes grew big as she confirmed, "Yes. It's the Alpha." She turned around and roundhouse kicked the Alpha, causing it to fall to the ground hard and giving her just enough time to reach the convoy. Once she did, she worked quickly to help the people.

Unfortunately, the Alpha quickly recovered and charged at Anna once again.

"Anna, you need to get out of there now," Patrick screamed.

All the while, Country never stopped shooting at it. "What's this thing made out of?!"

Anna thought to herself, "If I try to fight the Alpha, the people will still be in danger with all of these hounds and crawlers around."

"We're not going to get her this time," Country said.

Anna looked at the survivors and said to them, "Stay close to me." She then looked at the Alpha, watching as it got closer and closer. She closed her eyes and prayed: "I have faith in You, Lord."

Out of nowhere, a loud roar reverberated throughout the land, causing the Alpha to stop moving. A huge figure stepped out from the darkness and walked past Anna. When she opened her eyes, she saw what made that roar.

It was none other than Pratigue! Pratigue, the white lion, has returned!

CHAPTER FIFTY-TWO
The Lion Returns

Country and Patrick were in awe. "Is that Pratigue?" Patrick asked.

"Look at the size of him!" Country exclaimed.

Anna's eyes filled with tears as she whispered his name: "Pratigue."

Pratigue wasn't alone, though. He brought with him a pack of lions that ran towards the hounds and nightcrawlers. Pratigue charged straight toward the Alpha.

"Oh! It's about to be on like Godzilla and Kong!" said Country.

"We're going to be dead and gone if we don't get out of here soon." Patrick felt the need to remind Country they were still in danger. "Anna, this is your chance to get out of here!"

Patrick's voice helped Anna snap out of her daze. She told the survivors to stay close to her as they made their way towards the safety of the team.

CHAPTER FIFTY-THREE
Squealing Like A Pig

As the survivors climbed into the truck, Country asked the question they all had since Pratigue came to their rescue: "How many antelopes has he been eating?!"

Anna smiled when she replied, "I don't know, but I'm so glad to see him."

"All I know is that Country better back this thing up so we can get out of here because that fight is coming right at us!" Patrick yelled.

"Oh, snap!" Country said as he put the truck in reverse and stepped on the gas.

The fight between Pratigue and the Alpha came uncomfortably close.

"Go! Go! Go!" Patrick yelled.

"I am!" screamed Country. "Will you stop yelling in my ear like a squealing pig?" He was able to get the truck turned around and headed back to camp as the lions fought off the hounds and crawlers.

Once they returned, Amaka told Anna that William had a plan to stop the elements.

"That's great!"

"But," Amaka continued, "there's one thing…"

"What's that?" Anna asked.

"One of the elements has yet to show itself: Water."

Anna went into deep thought before saying, "Put me through to the ark."

"Admiral Stevenson, sir, we have an incoming call from Anna."

"Put her through." Once connected, he asked her, "What is it, Anna?"

"Tell me this: Are there any strange going-ons there in the water?"

"Not as far as I can tell. Why?"

"We believe the water elemental is in your area," replied Anna.

"Okay. We will be…" Before the Admiral could finish speaking, sirens started sounding in the ark's control deck.

A team member yelled, "A gate just opened in the country of Chad! It's enormous! It's classified as a colossal!" Just then, another siren sounded. "Oh, my goodness! Another gate just opened!"

"Where is that one?" Anna yelled into the radio.

"Here in the Red Sea, and it, too, is a colossal gate!" The suddenness of the activity obviously frazzled Admiral Stevenson. He told the remainder of the team on the ark, the Mako team, to prepare for underwater combat.

As team Mako—led by Gala—started diving into the water, they observed something in front of the gate. Gala radioed the ark. "Admiral, do you see this?"

"It's the water elemental," replied Admiral Stevenson. He then called Anna. "We found the water elemental. It's here—right in front of us."

CHAPTER FIFTY-FOUR
Great Faith

Anna and her team were facing their biggest challenge to date. With all the other teams scattered and engaging in fierce battles of their own, they also had to contend with not one but two colossal gates. The East's team was dealing with the gate in Chad, and the Mako team with the one in the Red Sea.

"What are we going to do?" asked Amaka.

Anna looked out into the darkness of the night, waiting for Pratigue to return before responding. "Contact the other arks and tell them what's going on, if they don't already know. In the meantime, we will go to Chad and do what we can until the rest of our team arrives."

"What if they won't be able to reach us? What about Pratigue?"

Anna looked Amaka in the eyes and said, "Have faith. Believe in our team. They will come. Don't worry about Pratigue, either. He will catch up soon enough."

CHAPTER FIFTY-FIVE
The Gates Are Opening

Meanwhile, on the other arks, their alarms were sounding as well, all because of the openings of the colossal gates. Gadin, Sonya, and Eion told all the sea team members on their arks to load up and head directly to the Red Sea for battle.

Eion whispered into the air, "Hold on, Sis. We're coming. Just hold on."

CHAPTER FIFTY-SIX
Close and Accurate

At the Red Sea, Gala contacted the Admiral. "Sir, we're picking up a swarm of leviathans coming right at us!"

"I know, Gala. We just have to hold out as long as we can. Help is coming."

A teammate said, "Sir, the Mako team is outnumbered. There are too many of them."

The Admiral spoke with confidence. "We will persevere."

"Okay, Mako team. Yes, we're outnumbered, but that doesn't matter. We have God on our side," Gala said. When the underwater battle began, she said, "This water elemental is going to be a problem. Is there anything from the North team on how to defeat them yet?"

"No. Not yet," Fen replied.

"Gala, the leviathans are heading towards the ark," another team member reported.

She got on the radio. "Hey, Admiral. You have unwanted guests coming your way."

"Thanks, Gala. We see them. Don't worry about us. We will handle them." The Admiral then told the others on the ark to prepare their defenses. "We must protect these people at all costs."

The water elemental started to form a giant whirlpool.

"It's trying to pull us and the ark in!" yelled Fen.

"Everyone find something to hold on to!" screamed Gala.

"Hold on to what?" Fen asked.

On the ark, a team member told the Admiral, "We're being pulling into the whirlpool!"

"Boost all engines to full power to try and pull away," he commanded.

With both the ark and the Mako team in danger of being sucked down the whirlpool, there was no way they could reach the gate to close it.

Gala then contacted the North team. "Guys, have you figured out how to stop them? We don't know how much longer we can hold out! We are in danger of being pulled into a giant whirlpool!"

"Oh, no," Zenny said. "Hey! Mako and the ark are in serious trouble. They're being sucked into a giant whirlpool made by the water elemental."

William clapped his hands and said, "Okay. I think I've figured out how to stop them. We fight element with element."

That response caused the entire North team to be confused.

"Umm… How do we do that?" asked Chibuzo.

"Let me explain. When an element interacts with a different type of element, it causes a chain reaction. In this case, we will have to use liquid nitrogen. I often wondered why our convoys had that and other types of chemicals. It just hit me that we were all given the tools necessary to deal with any type of situation we would face. So, in order to defeat the elementals, we must use the chemical elements we already have. Liquid nitrogen can neutralize fire, and the air will consume all the oxygen around them, suffocating them and making the water turn into steam, which will evaporate the elemental. For the earth and wood elementals, that chemical would not affect them. It would just roll off like water on a duck's back because both of those elements can survive in the coldest temperature. For them, we will have to use that special type of acid we use to cut and melt down the angelic metal." William paused before continuing. "But here's the dangerous part."

"I knew there was a 'but' coming," commented Osumara.

"We must get them to use their full power in order for them to show their true form. When they are gathering more energy, that's our only shot. We must attack when they are most vulnerable—and we have to get close enough and be accurate. With only two minutes to do it, if we miss, it may not work again because they will figure out what we are up to."

"Are you sure that tactic will work?" asked Chibuzo, obviously concerned about the plan.

"I know it will. That is why I am here," William replied.

"Okay! That's all I needed to hear! Zenny, contact all the teams and tell them what to do to defeat the elementals."

"Will do!"

CHAPTER FIFTY-SEVEN
Adriam and Hadeon

While all the teams began receiving details from the North team about how to defeat the elementals, the East team was close to reaching the country of Chad.

"Great job, North team!" Anna commended.

"Look at the size of that gate!" Amaka was amazed.

"We have incoming!" yelled Patrick.

"Prepare for battle, team!" Anna screamed.

Suddenly, something struck their convoy, causing it to tumble.

"What just hit us?" asked Country.

"Is everyone okay?" Anna asked, shaking her head to remove the shock. The others in the other convoys contacted them, asking if they were alright. "Everyone is saying they're okay. We're just trying to figure out what hit us."

"Look!" yelled Amaka.

"Everyone out! NOW!" screamed Anna. "Hurry!"

They scrambled to get out. Thankfully, it was just in time because something hit the convoy again, completely destroying it.

Once the smoke cleared, the team saw two beings that looked identical, with an army of night creepers close by.

"Those are the geminate twins," Anna said. "Their names are Adriam and Hadeon. Both names mean 'destroyer.' They are half-human/half-demon and children of Azel. The father is unknown, but rumors are he is the devil head of hate. The twins are very strong and skillful, and they command not just night creepers, but other demons as well."

The twins busted out in laughter, saying, "This is as far as you go, you weak fleshlings!"

"This is not good," Amaka murmured. "Those crazy demon twins are blocking our way."

"It's all good. We just have to push our way right through them!" Anna said confidently.

The geminate twins gave the signal to attack.

"Here they come!" yelled Patrick.

As the two opposing forces engaged, Anna noticed the geminates were trying to take out Amaka. She intervened, saving her teammate.

"Well, well, well. What do we have here, brother? Oh. I see. She is one of those special warriors," said Adriam.

Anna took out her crimson red nun chucks and said to them, "Yeah. I'm one of THOSE types!"

Hadeon charged at her, with Adriam close behind. Anna was able to strike them both with her weapon, but they still managed to cut her a little. "This isn't going to be easy. They were able to cut me somehow," she said to herself.

"Uh oh, brother. We better be careful with this one," Hadeon teased.

The others were still battling the demons and night creepers. "There has to be thousands of these things!" Patrick yelled.

"I know, and they're going to keep coming as long as that gate remains open!" Country yelled back.

"Hey, guys. We can do this! We just have to hold out until help arrives," Amaka stated.

CHAPTER FIFTY-EIGHT
Battling the Fire

Once all the teams were told how to defeat the elementals, they started making plans on taking them down.

The South team remained surrounded by both the fire and the hounds. Kemaah was trying to figure out a way to reach the fire elemental. "Alright. Listen. We have one tank of liquid nitrogen because we had to leave the rest behind. We will have to somehow get him, her, or whatever it is to get the fire burning even stronger so that it can take on its real form. Our suits can withstand almost any level of heat, but the beast also knows how to penetrate our gear."

"Okay, but what about the hounds that will be on us in minutes?" asked Nuo.

"While all of you are holding off the hounds, I will be the one trying to get to it so I can use the nitrogen."

"That's insane!" exclaimed Cole.

"Look. This will be our one and only shot. We need everyone to fight those hounds while I get that thing to disperse more fire."

"Well, we better load up our weapons because the hounds are here!" shouted Kane.

The fire elemental opened a pathway for the hounds to go through. At the same time, it shot a flaming dagger at the team.

"Wow. I guess we now know how it can take us out," Kane said.

"The plan is still the same. Raise your protection gear to full power. When I give the signal, attack the hounds while I go for the elemental." When Kemaah gave the signal, the team began shooting the hounds, and he went after the fire elemental.

"Kemaah, you better come back to us!" Kane called after him.

CHAPTER FIFTY- NINE
The Raging Flames

Kemaah ran towards the elemental to draw attention to him and away from the rest of the team. The elemental started sending out multiple burning daggers towards Kemaah. He tried to deflect and dodge the daggers that came at him. He could feel the temperature rising, just as one of the daggers hit him in the shoulder, causing him to fall to the ground.

The team was still holding off the hounds but heard Kemaah yell from being hit.

Nuo screamed, "Kemaah! Are you okay? We're coming!"

"NO! Stay there!"

The elemental then started throwing burning daggers at the team, almost hitting Chidike. Kemaah jumped and hollered, regaining the elemental's attention. "Hey! Hey! I'm the one you should be concerned about!"

Just then, the fire grew bigger.

"It's working!" Kemaah yelled.

As he got closer, the fire grew angrier, and its fire grew larger. It released a huge burst of flames at Kemaah.

"Get down!" he screamed to his team as the raging flames came right at them, consuming the hounds. Kemaah saw the elemental's true form through the fire: a human with burn scars all over. "I see you now!" He moved fast as he could through the flames to throw the liquid nitrogen. "I must hurry," he said to himself. "The two minutes are almost up, and the fire will soon reach the survivors in the truck!"

The elemental saw Kemaah coming and prepared to enter its full fire form. Before it could, though, Kemaah threw the liquid nitrogen and then shot the container, causing it to explode and expel its contents directly on the elemental. "I got you!" yelled Kemaah. The contents instantly suffocated the fire elemental, just as William said it would. "Ha! You burnt up your dogs!" he taunted.

In a matter of seconds, the elemental was completely consumed by the nitrogen, and the fire quickly dissipated. Both the fire elemental and the hounds were defeated!

Sadly, as a result of the battle, Kemaah suffered severe burns on his left arm. As he walked back to the others, Kane approached him and said, "Bro, are you okay? Your arm looks bad."

"Yeah. I'm okay," he replied as Nuo came to him as well and provided medical attention. After Nuo fixed him up, Kemaah said, "Let's go. We must get these people to safety and head to Chad to help the others."

CHAPTER SIXTY
The Teams Come Together

In the Congo, the Central team was in a fierce battle with the wood elemental. They were taking heavy losses in the process.

"We're getting killed out here!" yelled Ryan.

"I know!" Dakini couldn't help but agree with him. "Hey, Bari! Do you have that chemical yet?"

"I'm working on it! I'm trying to get it out of the convoy, but it's tightly wedged in there!"

Mizzy ran to give him a hand. "I'll help you."

"We must be careful not to spill any on us," Bari instructed.

Meanwhile, the wood elemental continued to attack with multiple branches, stabbing the team and the gorillas and making it difficult to fight against the nightcrawlers.

In what seemed like the nick of time, Mizzy yelled, "We got it!"

Bari put the unique chemical into a capsule-type bullet in a special gun. "It's ready!"

"Okay. Good. Now, all we have to do is get that thing to use its full power somehow," Dakini stated.

Ryan offered a suggestion. "How about we each come at it from a different direction? That should make it mad enough to want to use its full power to try and take us all at out once."

"That could work," said Bari.

"Okay! Let's do it while the gorillas are holding back the crawlers. We need to stop it now!" Dakini yelled.

The team strategically came at the wood elemental from all sides, and their plan worked. It got predictably angry because it couldn't hit any of them.

"It's working!" Dakini shouted happily. "Keep it up!"

"It's not enough, though," Bari said. "More crawlers are coming. The gorillas won't be able to hold them off much longer. We lost too many of our guys to come at it the way we want to."

Suddenly, more shots began hitting the elemental.

"We're here!" shouted Kemaah.

"It's the South team! Alright. We can definitely take it down now!" Ryan yelled.

The South and Central teams hit the elemental from all sides, causing it to use its full power. The Congo jungle seemed to come alive, as giant roots protruded from the ground, and branches came from everywhere.

"Everyone, look out!" yelled Bari.

The team worked hard to evade the deadly branches and roots. Just then, Ryan saw the baby gorilla about to get killed by one of the branches and ran to save it.

"Ryan! Get out of there!" yelled Dakini. "Do you see the opening you need, Bari?"

"I see it!" he yelled in response, but before he could take a shot, a branch knocked the gun out of his hand.

Ryan managed to save the baby gorilla, but as soon as he grabbed it, a branch with a special metal at the tip that could pierce the team's suits stabbed him in the stomach.

"Nooo!" yelled Dakini.

Everyone looked at the scene before them with sadness.

"Where is the gun with the chemicals?" Mizzy screamed.

"It was knocked out of my hand," Bari replied.

Dakini said, "We need to find it fast before time runs out and it changes back!"

Kemaah asked her, "What are you looking for?"

"A special gun that has the acid chemical bullet in it."

The team tried desperately to locate the gun. Time was running out.

"As long as all these roots and branches remain in our way, it's going to be hard to find it!" shouted Mizzy. Little did they know, the gun was lying just a few feet in front of her.

The elemental caused roots to start wrapping up everyone on the ground.

"This is not good," Nuo said. "Time is almost gone."

After the elemental finished, it then launched branches at the team in an attempt to kill them all.

It was then when Ryan realized the gun was in front of Mizzy, so he gathered all his remaining strength and crawled to grab the weapon—fighting the roots that held him captive the entire way. Once he had the gun in his hand, he stood, aimed it at the elemental, and said, "I see you now." He then shot the acid-filled bullet, hitting the elemental square in its chest. Instantly, the wood elemental began to dissolve, and the roots released their captives.

Ryan fell to the ground, and the baby gorilla stood over him, trying to get him to get up. The other gorillas came to him as well.

Dakini ran over to Ryan. "Ryan, stay with us."

Barely able to speak, he asked, "Are you, the others, and the baby gorilla okay?"

"Yes."

"Good. I'm glad. I think I need just to rest a little. Okay?"

As everyone stood around him, they were saddened, for they knew their friend was about to die.

"Go ahead and get some rest, Ryan," Dakini said.

Ryan slowly closed his eyes and passed away.

The team was distraught as they looked around and saw their fallen comrades and some of the gorillas lying lifeless. Although they succeeded in destroying the wood elemental, they lost many good people and furry friends in the process.

As the team began to gather their friends, Dakini announced, "No one is to be left behind."

"Are you okay?" Keemah asked Dakini.

"No. Not really. Thanks for helping us. I don't know what would have happened if y'all hadn't shown up."

"It's all good. You know how we do."

Once everyone was accounted for, the team continued on, with the gorillas following them. Once they reached the edge of the jungle, the gorillas stopped.

As the team turned to look at them, Dakini said, "Thank you for helping us." The gentle beasts gave the group their best look that said, "You're welcome," before turning around and walking back into the jungle. The silverback remained for a moment longer, beating his chest as if to say, "Stay strong and win!" He then turned away and joined the others.

"Wow! It looks like you made some good friends," Kemaah said.

"More than you will ever know," replied Dakini.

With the South and Central teams successful in their missions, it was time to head East to aid that team.

CHAPTER SIXTY-ONE
It May Be the Last

In the West, Comfort's team devised a dangerous plan to try and get the earth elemental to make a huge earthquake — one that could easily wipe out her entire team.

"Hey, you know I'm down for whatever," Nahara said, "but if we're going to do this, we need to do it now."

"Chrissy, do you have that special chemical compound ready yet?" asked Vincent.

"Yeah. It's ready."

"Tell everyone to hit it with everything they have — and I mean hit it hard," Comfort instructed. "Even if it turns itself into a diamond, it will still have to use its full power because of all the force it will be taking from our weapons."

"You do know when it uses its full power and causes a major earthquake that we may not survive," Nahara said with concern.

"I know, but we have no choice," Comfort stated. She then radioed all the teams. "Hey, guys. This is Comfort. I'm radioing in because this may very well be our last battle. In order to defeat the earth elemental, we must make it cause a major earthquake."

Everyone listened in and was filled with sadness as they thought about Comfort and her team's possible outcome.

He continued. "We here in the West are prepared to do what must be done to win against this entity."

Anna listened with frustration, knowing there was nothing she could do to help them.

"So, to everyone, I say: Keep on fighting, and may God be with us all," Comfort said before ending the transmission.

The West team then began their plan of attack to defeat the earth elemental.

"Put it on that thing!" Nahara yelled.

Just as Comfort directed, they started hitting the elemental with everything they had. Once it changed into a diamond form, it became immobile and grew increasingly angry. It was then it started using its full power. The ground began to shake violently.

"Here we go!" shouted Vincent.

"Get ready, Chrissy!" Comfort yelled.

As expected, the entire country shook. Out of concern, some of the other teams tried to contact the West team but received nothing but the sound of static in return.

CHAPTER SIXTY-TWO
Where There's Music...

"Well, well, well. It looks like your friends are about to be killed by the elemental," the geminate twins taunted.

"Shut up!" Anna said as she continued to battle them.

Then, as quickly as the earthquake started, it came to an abrupt end. When the teams tried to contact those in the West, no sound came in return. The line of communication was silent.

The air and water elementals both stopped their assault, as if they knew fire, wood, and earth had been defeated. With that new reality, they grew enraged, and both unleashed their full power. They did not realize that the North and the Mako teams had already begun their attacks and were inspired by the other teams' victories.

As the last two elements showed their true form, they were revealed as humans. Both teams were also victorious against their opponents, but sadly, they lost many of their teammates along the way.

The time finally came to focus all energies on closing the colossal gates.

"Aww! What's wrong? Are you about to cry because your friends are dead?" the geminate twins teased.

Anna was unmoved. "You lost your friends, too. All the elementals have been defeated."

"We don't care about them. We knew they weren't going to survive. They were weak and more of a distraction."

Anna stared hard at the twins and was just about to attack them again when she felt a hand on her shoulder and a voice that said, "What's up, sis?" She turned her head and saw it was Eion beside her.

"Where did you come from?" asked the geminates. True to twins' nature, they often spoke in unison.

Eion ignored them.

"What's up, bro?" Anna said with a happy sigh.

"It's going to be okay, Anna. We're here," Eion replied.

"I hear music," Country said, "and where there's music, there's that crazy Crae Crae!"

As Crae approached, he replied, "And you know this, bro!"

Anna looked all around her. Not only had Eion and his team joined her; all the teams from every ark had arrived, including all the Mako teams.

One of the teammates reported to the Admiral. "Sir, all the teams are here, except for those who are with the East team."

"Good. Now we just need to close these gates."

Gala smiled happily. "I sure am glad to see y'all!"

"We got you, Gala," Brad said. When he finally turned around and saw the opened gate, his jaw dropped. "Whoa! Is that the colossal gate?"

"Yep. That's it," replied Gala.

As the sea team gathered together, they looked at the gate in awe and the immense number of leviathans that floated in front of it.

"Guys, it's up to us to close that gate down here while the others are up there trying to do the same. Now, let's win this!" yelled Admiral Stevenson.

"Well, team. You heard the Admiral! Let's go fight these leviathans!" Brad shouted.

An underwater battle, unlike any other, was about to go down.

CHAPTER SIXTY-THREE
The Momma Witch

On land, Anna and Eion were about to go toe-to-toe with the geminate twins.

"Who let you two out of the house?" Eion taunted. "Oh. Never mind. I know who your crazy mother is."

"Where is your witch of a momma?" Anna asked. "We know Azel is alive and what she is planning."

"You won't see it because you will be dead!" replied Adriam.

The geminates then attacked Anna and Eion, engaging in a battle with an ending for the ages.

CHAPTER SIXTY-FOUR
Meet the Mate

Meanwhile, the East team and the Renegades were in a fierce battle, trying to reach the gate.

"The other teams from the arks are on the way," said a teammate.

"Good!" replied Patrick. "The South, Central, and North teams are on the way, too."

"Well, there's a lot of something coming through the gate," said Amaka.

"Uh oh. Here comes more!" Hadeon said with a laugh.

"It doesn't matter how many come out of that gate. We will still defeat you and close both gates!" Anna shouted.

"Sis, we need to hurry and finish this so that we can go help the others," Eion said.

Suddenly, something strange emerged from the gate.

"What is that?!" asked Crae.

"No. It can't be," Country said.

"Can't be what, Country?" When no response came, Crae asked again, "Can't be what?!" The tone of his voice grew progressively concerned and louder.

"It's another Alpha, with a horde of hounds, nightcrawlers, and Dominions." Patrick was the one who answered Crae's question.

"But wait. Pratigue is still fighting one," said Amaka, "unless this one is its mate."

"No way," Anna said with an obvious look of surprise.

"What is it?" asked Eion. "What is that thing?"

"It's an Alpha for sure, but how can that be? Pratigue is fighting one in the Serengeti." Anna's response was filled with confusion.

"Pratigue? He's in Africa?" Eion asked.

"Yes. He saved me from the Alpha, which is why I don't know what this one is."

"Why the grim look?" said the geminates. "Meet the mother Alpha!"

"Dude! We are about to be destroyed!" said Patrick.

"Bring it on!" yelled Crae.

The mother Alpha charged at the warriors with the other creatures right behind it. Anna and Eion were still fighting the evil twins.

"Keep fighting, Anna!" Eion shouted. "This battle must be won!"

CHAPTER SIXTY-FIVE
A Full Onslaught

All of a sudden, a boisterous roar came out of nowhere. Just as it happened with the other Alpha, the mother Alpha and geminate twins stopped attacking the warriors.

"What was that?" asked the twins.

The warriors knew exactly what it was. A big smile spread across Anna's face. Eion noticed and asked, "That's Pratigue, isn't it?"

"You will see."

"Crae, my man. You're about to see something cray-cray!" Country said as a knowing smile spread across his face, too. As soon as he said that, packs of lions came running past them, with Pratigue in the lead.

Eion watched with amazement and joy. "All I can say right now is WHOA!"

"I know, right?" Anna agreed. She then looked back at the evil twins and said, "You know we're about to kick your tail, right?"

For the first time since engaging in battle, the twins were truly fearful for just a moment before saying, "This doesn't change a thing." They then resumed their fight with Anna and Eion.

Amazingly, the lions weren't the only ones that came. Fighter jets from all the arks joined the war, shooting and killing Dominions, along with the Central, South, North, and West teams.

"Yeah, baby! Yeah!" yelled Crae.

Anna was surprised to see the arrival of the West team.

"We're here, Anna!" Comfort said as she embraced her in a hug.

"But how?"

"Didn't I tell you everything was going to be okay?" Eion stated matter-of-factly.

CHAPTER SIXTY-SIX
They're Saved!

So, just how did the West team survive? Well…

As the team was battling the earth elemental and just when it made use of its full power that caused the massive earthquake, Gadin and Sonya arrived. Each stood on opposite sides of the elemental and punched their fists into the ground, showing just how strong they were and keeping the land from splitting apart with their countermove.

****

Gadin yelled, "Hurry, guys!"

"Hurry! Do it now, Chrissy!" yelled Sonya. "We don't know how long we can hold it together!"

"Go now!" Comfort screamed at Vincent.

As they fought their way through and finally made it to the elemental — which turned out to be a female — it looked at them and shook her head with tears forming in her eyes. Chrissy lowered the weapon.

The elemental spoke softly. "It's okay. Do it."

"I'll do it, Chrissy. Give it to me," Vincent demanded. She handed him the special chemical compound. "I'm sorry. May God have mercy on your soul." He then shot the chemical into the elemental, destroying her and saving everyone.

Afterward, Vincent and Chrissy felt oddly bad for the elemental as Comfort congratulated them.

"Great job, you two," Gadin said with glee.

Sonya agreed. "Yeah! Great work! Don't' feel bad. We saw the darkness that was in her. There was nothing we could've done for her, okay?"

"I know," said Vincent. "It just doesn't feel right."

"Evil likes to prey on the young," Gadin said. "That's why we're trying to make sure it doesn't continue."

"Well, if it weren't for the two of you showing up, we wouldn't be here," Comfort stated with gratefulness in her voice.

Sonya reminded them all, "We are a team. Right now, the others need us ASAP!"

After the victory, the West team left immediately to meet up with the others.

CHAPTER SIXTY-SEVEN
The Gate Is the Focus

"Comfort! Y'all made it!" Kemaah said, greeting his friend with a hug.

"Yeah, thanks to Gadin and Sonya!"

"Where's Anna?" asked Gadin.

"She and Eion are fighting the geminate twins," replied Amaka.

"Okay. I'm sure they have things handled. We need to focus on destroying that gate," Gadin said.

"Right," said Sonya, "because Azel has already set one of the devil heads free—'Wrath.' We don't want her to free another one!"

As everyone focused their attacks on the demons that blocked the gate, the Red Sea underwater battle intensified.

CHAPTER SIXTY-EIGHT
Unleash It All

"They're coming from everywhere, Gala!" yelled Fen.

"I know! Try to stay focused!"

"Melendez, watch out!" Brad screamed. "You have five around you!"

"I got them, bro! Thanks!"

The Admiral spoke to Gala. "I'm going to focus all of the ark's fire right down the center. That should give you all a shot to reach the gate."

"Okay! Go for it! We're ready!"

"FIRE ALL WEAPONS!" yelled the Admiral.

The ark unleashed all its weapons on the leviathans, making way for all the sea team to go on the offensive to close the gate.

"That's it! Let's go!" Brad shouted.

As the sea team made their way, they received a call from the ark. "Stop. Wait." Said a team member.

"What's wrong?" asked the Admiral.

"Sir, I just picked up something from within the gate. It's enormous…and it's coming!"

The sea team stopped, wondering why they were being delayed. "Talk to me," said Gala.

"All sea team members withdraw! Repeat! Withdraw!" yelled the Admiral in a panic. "Something big is coming!"

In a flash, it came through the gate.

"Oh, my God!" Gala exclaimed.

"Is that what I think it is?" asked the Admiral.

A giant leviathan that equaled the size of the ark emerged from the gate.

"Let him have it!" commanded the Admiral. "Unleash everything we have left on that thing!"

No matter what the team did, the giant leviathan kept coming at them.

"Ark Three! This is Gadin. Admiral Stevenson needs immediate support!"

"We are on the way to their location now. Admiral, this is Ark Three. We are just a few minutes away from your location."

"Good! We're going to need your help!" the Admiral replied.

CHAPTER SIXTY-NINE
Angelic Vs. Evil Armor

"I don't see Azel yet," said Sonya.

"I know, but we can't worry about that right now. If we don't close these colossal gates, it's over," Gadin responded.

The underwater battle was coming to a climactic end, as the Admiral attempted to ram the giant leviathan with the ark.

"Tell everyone to hold on," commanded the Admiral. "We're about the ram that thing!"

One of the teammates got on the intercom and instructed everyone to hold on to something. "It's about to get rough!" To Gala and the sea team, he said, "Get out of the way! We're going to ram the leviathan back into the gate!"

Just then, Ark Three arrived. They, too, joined the onslaught and launched everything they had at the leviathan. "What is that thing made out of? We barely put a scratch on it!"

"I know," replied the Admiral, "but I have a plan. I want everyone to hit it with all you got to push it back closer to the gate. Then, we're going to ram it back inside."

"Okay. But do you think the ark can handle it?" asked a team member on Ark Three.

"It has to. It's the only way it can be done," replied the Admiral.

"Okay!" came the response from Ark Three. "We are with you, sir!"

"Alright, everyone. When I give the signal, fire at it all at once!" When the Admiral gave the signal, the firing began, pushing the giant leviathan closer to the gate. Then, with the ark going at full speed, the Admiral made his move.

Everyone watched in suspense.

"Come on… Come on… It has to work," Gala said to herself.

The giant leviathan saw the ark heading straight for it and chose to go head-to-head with its opponent. The smaller leviathans tried to stop the ark's progress but couldn't. They were simply destroyed on impact due to the force of the ark's high speed.

The Admiral looked at the giant leviathan and said to no one in particular, "Okay, buddy. Let's see if your armor is stronger than our angelic armor!" He then instructed the crew members to brace themselves for the upcoming impact.

As the ark and giant leviathan collided, the impact was so strong, it caused a huge underwater shockwave that caused the tide to rise and the entire country to shake.

"Hold on, everyone!" Gala yelled.

Ark Three used all of its engines' forces to keep those in the water from spinning out of control.

The Admiral's plan worked! The giant leviathan was no match for the ark. The collision caused it, and the others like it, to go flying back into the gate.

CHAPTER SEVENTY
The Necessary Sacrifice

On land, everyone felt the ground beneath their feet shake.

"What the heck was that?" asked Crae. "It sounded like something ran into the side of a mountain!"

Once the underwater battle's effects began to subside, even though the plan worked, the Admiral's ark was still damaged.

"We have water breaches coming from everywhere, sir," a team member reported.

"Take us to the top and begin to abandon ship," the Admiral ordered. "Ark Three, I hope you have room!"

"Yes, sir. We have plenty. Plus, the other arks are inbound as well."

There was a need to hurry with the evacuation because the ark was starting to sink.

Gala contacted the Admiral. "The gate is still open, and more leviathans will soon return."

The Admiral knew they would not survive another attack, so he told the sea team to hurry and board Ark Three immediately. He told them, "I am going to set the ark on self-destruct and send it sailing into the gate. With the size of the ark, it should be able to close it once and for all."

"Okay," replied Gala as she instructed her team to board Ark Three.

One of the teammates asked the Admiral, "How are you going to make the ark go into the gate and self-destruct? The auto-pilot is damaged."

"I know, son. You just make sure everyone is on Ark Three. That's an order."

The teammate looked at him with sadness and replied, "Okay, sir." It was apparent to the teammate what was on the Admiral's mind.

CHAPTER SEVENTY-ONE
Giants Return

As the remaining team members scrambled to board Ark Three, the others on land were soon to encounter something big—something they have never seen but heard about.

"Yo! Something's coming out of the gate!" yelled Amaka.

Not one, but two giants stepped out of the gate. Everyone watched in shock, as most of them have never seen a giant before. Gadin and Sonya, however, knew exactly what they were.

"It's the Rephaims," Sonya said.

Rephaims were a race of giants that are said to exist back in the Bible days.

"I thought they were extinct," Gadin replied.

"That witch probably has something to do with them showing up here."

Gadin shook his head. "Well, we better deal with them fast before more of them come out."

Sonya instructed everyone to steer clear from the giants.

"Giants?! Are you kidding me? What else is going to come out of that gate?" Patrick asked sarcastically.

"I don't know, but we must seal that gate quickly," replied Country.

CHAPTER SEVENTY-TWO
They're Coming Soon

Meanwhile, Anna and Eion's battle against the geminate twins was concluding, with the twins gloating because of the two giants' appearance. "We told you there's nothing any of you can do. It looks like mother has sent the Rephaims."

"Shut up!" Anna said. "I don't know why you're gloating!"

"She's right," Eion added. "This fight is about to be OVER!"

Beaten and frustrated, the twins knew they were right as they witnessed Pratigue defeat the other Alpha. He then joined Gadin and Sonya to fight the two giants.

"This ends now," said Anna.

The twins were desperate. They tried to trick Anna and Eion by trying to get in their heads to cause confusion, but that tactic didn't work on them.

"Ha! You really thought that would work on my brother and me? We are immune to mind tricks, you idiots!"

Simultaneously, the brother-sister team pulled out their weapons and ended the twins' lives. Before they died, they started speaking about the coming of the Nephilims.

"The what, you evil brats? What are you talking about?" demanded Anna. No other words were spoken.

"They're gone, sis. We need to go help the others now."

CHAPTER SEVENTY-THREE
The Weak Spot

At virtually the same time Anna and Eion arrived, two more Rephiams came out.

"Well, which one do you want, sis?" Eion asked with a laugh.

The brother-sister team clashed with the giants. Pratigue jumped on one of the giant's back while the other lions attacked its legs.

"That's it, Pratigue! Now, watch out!" Gadin yelled. He then ran and jumped high into the air, punching the giant in the face, sending it to the ground.

Sonya grabbed the other giant by the leg and swung it around, throwing it into a building and then hitting it in the forehead, killing it. "Their weak spot is the middle of their forehead," she yelled.

Gadin then punched the giant he was fighting in the forehead, causing its demise.

"Pratigue! Go help Anna and Eion," shouted Gadin.

Eion and Anna heard Sonya when she told where the giants' weak spots were and prepared to kill the other two with the help of the Pratigue and the packs of lions.

CHAPTER SEVENTY-FOUR
Shut It Down

"Guys, I found the source of the dark energy that opens the gates!" Comfort reported.

"Where is it?" asked Crae.

"Underneath that building up there." Comfort directed everyone's attention to a three-story abandoned building.

"She's right," agreed William. "That's where there's the most activity."

"Well, let's go and shut it down, then," Country said with some exasperation.

"It's dangerous, though," said Comfort.

"We know, but it has to be done." Country then turned and started walked toward the building, not looking back to see if his team was following. However, he was pleased when Comfort, Crae, William, and a few others joined him. They battled their way into the building and down to the lower floor to detonate and destroy the energy source.

CHAPTER SEVENTY-FIVE
Thank You for Your Service

Back at the Red Sea, everyone was safe aboard Ark Three and quickly distanced themselves from the area as they watched the damaged ark begin its journey to the gate.

"Wait a minute. Where's Admiral Stevenson?" asked Gala.

"He's on the ark," replied a teammate.

"What?!" Gala yelled. "Why didn't you stop and bring him to me?" She was hysterical and tried to get off the ark to save him. The team, however, stopped her.

"I tried, but since the auto-pilot was damaged and someone needed to direct the ark manually, he wouldn't let me stop him. He gave me a direct order to make sure everyone got off the ark safely."

Gala screamed into the radio, "NO! NO! NO, ADMIRAL! GET OUT OF THERE! PLEASE!"

He replied, "You know that's not possible, Gala. I am very blessed and honored to be a part of this. You all saved me and then made me Admiral of your amazing ark. I will be forever grateful that my life's journey will end this way. You all must continue the battle—and win. Please tell Anna she is a lot stronger than she thinks and is an awesome team leader. God be with you all."

The communication between the two arks fell silent.

Gala then whispered, "Thank you for your service, Admiral."

CHAPTER SEVENTY-SIX
Another One Destroyed

As everyone aboard Ark Three watched the ark go into the gate from a safe distance, a bright light was released, followed by a massive explosion.

On land, the team felt the ground shake once again.

"What in the world was that?" asked Patrick.

"Another colossal gate has been destroyed!" announced Amaka. "They did it!"

Anna stood in place, quiet and perfectly still. Eion approached her and asked, "What's wrong?"

"Something horrible just happened." Right then, someone reported the other colossal gate was destroyed.

"Hey, sis. That's great, right? What could be wrong?"

"Something's not right. I can feel it but can't put my finger on what it is yet."

CHAPTER SEVENTY-SEVEN
Two More Gone

On the lower floor of the building, Country and the others also heard the news about the gates.

"Yes! They did it!" Crae said. "Now, it's our turn."

"Well, we have demons coming!" shouted William.

"We'll hold them back while y'all go place the detonators," said Crae.

As Crae and the others fought the demons, the building became unstable and began to crumble.

"We must get out of here now! This place is about to crumble and seal us in!" yelled William.

"Okay! Everyone get out! Now!" Country commanded.

Patrick radioed Anna and told her about the plan to seal the energy source.

"Okay. I'm coming to help," she said—but then she saw some of them running out. As they were running, some of the building fell on top of Country and Comfort, trapping them inside.

Crae tried to dig them out. "I'm not leaving y'all behind!"

"Bro! Go!" yelled Country. "Anna and the others need you. Now, go!"

Comfort echoed Country's sentiment. "It's okay. Go!"

Crae didn't want to leave them but knew he had to. As he ran outside, he met Anna and told her what happened. She immediately contacted them. "I'm coming!"

"No, Anna," Comfort said. "There's no time. The gate needs to be closed now! Anna, remember: It's up to you and the others. We have always believed in y'all ever since Eziah told us about you. Now, go meet up with the others and win!"

Country and Comfort looked at each other with tears in their eyes. Country then grabbed Comfort's hands and said to her, "It's going to be okay. God is with us." He then radioed Crae and told him, "Never stop playing those beats, bro." Those were his last words before setting off the detonators.

Everyone ran a safe distance away and, just as before, a bright light formed, followed by a massive explosion, closing the gate. The team watched with sadness as they knew they lost two of their good friends.

CHAPTER SEVENTY-EIGHT
To the Safe Zone

Gala contacted Anna.

"I take it you managed to close the gate?" Anna asked.

"Yeah," Gala replied with sadness in her voice.

Afraid of the answer but needing to ask anyway, Anna asked, "Did everyone make it?"

"No. We had some casualties, including Admiral Stevenson. He was the one who destroyed the gate."

All the team members listened to the somber news.

Anna walked away from the team with tears in her eyes. Eion was about to go after her but was stopped by Sonya. "I think we need to let her be for now," she said gently.

Although the teams were successful in their missions, they lost a lot of friends along the way. After all the arks met up, they brought all the survivors of Africa together onto the arks. Even Pratigue and the other lions accompanied them onto the arks.

As Anna rubbed Pratigue, both sad and grateful at the same time, she said to him, "I'm so glad you are here and coming with us. The others will be delighted to see you."

As they set off, everyone watched as the view of Africa's coastline shrunk as they floated further away. Each member of the team reminisced about the battles they faced and the friends they lost. Their final mission was to meet up with the others in the safe zone.

CONCLUSION

Although the gates were closed, it was not safe with Azel, the creepers, and then nightcrawlers still lurking around. The teams were victorious…or so they thought.

As soon as they were out of sight, Azel appeared with Wrath.

"Your children have been killed," he said.

"They were weak," Azel replied. However, deep down, she felt a little sad for her children, but not enough to lose her focus on what she came to do. "I knew they were not strong enough to deal with them, but they served their purpose. They kept the warriors away long enough for me to gather the devil heads."

Azel then summoned ten more devil heads and said to them, "Unleash the Nephilims and send them to the safe zone!"

Azel has gathered the devil heads and unleashed a race of Nephilims—beings that are half-angel/half-human, thought to be extinct, and more powerful than even the strongest demons in Hell—to the safe zone to wage war against the safe zone.

****

Meanwhile, somewhere unknown, a man was waking up from a deep slumber.

"He's finally waking up," whispered a voice.

As the man slowly opened his eyes, he asked, "Where am I? What's going on?"

"Hello, Josh. My name is Eziah, and there is much we need to discuss with very little time."

Josh is alive. What plan does Eziah have for him? Will he even choose to join Eziah?

More will be revealed as the battle for humanity continues in *Spiritual Warriors: Darkest 'Til Dawn!*

RELEASING IN 2021

Follow Author Nakia L. Brown @
Twitter: KBmind75
Instagram: kbmind75

9 781948 853101